Samuél Lopez-Barrantes

Slim and The Beast

Kingdom Anywhere Publishing
Paris, France

First published in the United States of America by Inkshares (2015)
10th Anniversary Edition published by Kingdom Anywhere (2025)

ISBN (paperback) 979-8-9895803-3-0
ISBN (eBook) 979-8-9895803-4-7

Cover Design: Saskia Meiling
Chapter Illustrations: Aaron Lopez-Barrantes
Edited by Augusta Sagnelli

For permissions or information, please contact:
kingdomanywherepub@gmail.com

for your former self

THE B.A.M LIST
WE'RE OPEN,
COME ON IN

Slim and The Beast

Ingredients

"To be sure, a human being is a finite thing, and his freedom is restricted. It is not freedom from conditions, but it is freedom to take a stand toward the conditions."
— Viktor Frankl

Slim's Famous Burger

Lettuce, coleslaw, sliced tomatoes, a burger patty, American cheese, avocado, a second patty, a fried egg, ketchup, and hot sauce—Texas Pete to be precise.

SLIM AND THE BEAST

1

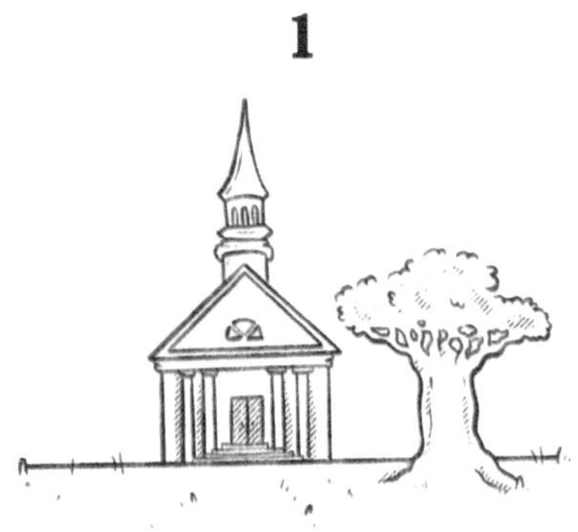

A Soldier & His Stalker

As I watched him lying in his own pool of blood, all I could think of was that half-eaten burger: lettuce, coleslaw, sliced tomatoes, a burger patty, American cheese, avocado, a second patty, a fried egg, ketchup and hot sauce—Texas Pete to be precise.

I'm going to tell you about a man named Slim. Who he is isn't important. It's who he was that matters now. He came from a time before your eye-pads and blue-tooths and tweeting pages—not too long ago but long enough to make a difference—from a time where if you wanted to get to know someone it wasn't through yellow smiles and little red hearts, but through honest conversation. The only kindle was to light a fire, the nicest cell phone was called a razor, and even though Facebook did exist, most people still made their friends at the bar. During that first decade of this here century, relationships took time and strayed from brevity. You went to bars for civilization, maybe some music and a bit of whiskey; sure, you could go for other reasons, too, but only the loneliest of folk went to be seen.

Slim wasn't one to shy away from attention, but he was self-conscious on account of his scar. He'd taken a bullet through the jugular during Operation Iraqi Freedom and lost faith in "the cause" during his second tour. He'd grown up as an afterthought of what some might call a deadbeat mother, and spent his formative years at Stoke Ridge Military Academy, where the pedophiliacally-inclined Sgt. Chandler Dykes obsessed over Slim's naked torso and the other cadets' sturdy frames. But *all in good time, little pretty*, as a wicked witch once said, *all in good time*.

Suffice to say Slim didn't enjoy his time at Stoke Ridge, not the least 'cause Sgt. Dykes was particularly fond of the kid, what with his sharp tongue and a proclivity for aggression. See, Dykes had a tendency toward self-pity, abusing Slim, and drinking Johnny Walker, and though he never showered with his cadets, I'd venture to say he thought about it a few times. Dykes was fond of convincing the young boys to do shirtless push-ups in his office, too. He didn't abuse 'em in a sexual way, at least I don't think, but it was certainly a sign of the times that most scars had to be seen to be believed.

But if I'm going to tell you about Slim's scars, I've got to take Dykes' scars into account, too, which were deep and invisible, more engrained somehow. He used Slim and the other cadets—"Dykes' Tykes" he called 'em, that well-toned troupe of at-risk youth—to help quell his demons, watching them pump out more shirtless push-ups than any cared to count. Under the insectan buzz of fluorescent light, Slim often fell asleep on the stale carpet of Dykes' office, too exhausted after the workout to move. And while the sergeant coveted all of his tykes, he was particularly fond of the skinny kid with a single name. Maybe it's 'cause Slim enjoyed doing push-ups, or perhaps 'cause Slim had a kind of fight about him. Whatever the reason, Dykes became obsessed, and it wasn't until the Welcome Back Heroes! event when Slim was nineteen, in that barren town of Stoke Ridge, North Carolina—the town's main attraction being a brick building with a white steeple—that this story either commenced or drew to a close, depending on your preference for happy endings.

The Welcome Back Heroes! event was a sign of things to come, for it was the day Slim reached the top of Sgt. Dykes' B.A.M. LIST. The Belligerents According to Me list, filled with the names of Dykes' mother, father, and other supposed enemies from his fallow past, was first displayed in his Stoke Ridge office—which, according to Slim, smelled like an unkempt microwave—and was later hung in the sergeant's home off Exit 263, in a one-story cabin with a rickety screen door, built on a once-fertile piece of land that's now hardened earth and brown grass.

"Welcome back, son," Dykes greeted the prodigal kid.

Just a few days prior to the Welcome Back Heroes! event Slim had been in Iraq on his first tour. The white bandage fresh around his neck had to be changed every evening. Slim stood with his hands behind his back to accept an award for *Outstanding Service to the Stoke Ridge Community and Nation as a Whole*. They stood on an elevated stage in the middle of the basketball court, the room packed with folks who hadn't yet heard of Slim, a true American hero's welcome.

"Congratulations on your medal." Dykes faked a smile

and spoke into the mic. "Good to have you back, now state your name and rank, son."

Dykes stuck out his hand. Slim didn't reciprocate. "I ain't your son, Chandler. Give me the mic."

Chairs scuffed the gym floor and Dykes' voice bounced off the bannerless rafters; the aluminum roofing rejected the echoes, sending them back down to the podium where Slim took control of the stage.

"What a pleasure it is, what a pleasure it is." Slim shook the sergeant's hand and gripped it tightly. "I hoped I'd never see you again, Chandler Dykes . . ."

Dykes was upset you see because Slim had called him by his first name *twice*. "Name and rank son—and you address me as sergeant."

"I'm a war hero now," Slim laughed. "More than you can say for yourself. Careful now Dykes. You don't want that forehead vein popping out . . ."

Dykes laughed nervously, trying to distract the audience. He put his arm around Slim as if it were a friendly conversation, turning away from the mic to say something in private.

Whatever Dykes whispered, Slim fell silent as Dykes turned back to the audience with a yellow-toothed smile.

"Sorry about that folks. Technical issues. Now give it up for Slim—our hero of Iraq!"

The audience applauded but they did not roar. Dykes tried to corral Slim. Slim didn't abide.

"Get your goddamn hands off of me," Slim said into the mic.

Dykes' face twitched. The audience squirmed. And

perhaps knowing their history, or perhaps 'cause he liked the spotlight, the academy's director—a bear of a man by the name of General Haith, who'd die in a house fire a few years down the line—scrambled onto the stage, took Slim's place on the podium, positioned his broad shoulders between Slim and Sgt. Dykes, and laughed loudly. The mic gave feedback. The video footage corroborates it. A child in the front row stuck his fingers in his ears; other spectators squinted at the stage as if staring at the sun, wincing from the feedback as they waited for what came next.

"Let's give it up for Slim!" General Haith boomed. "Our hometown hero. Maybe the finest soldier we've ever had!"

The tension escaped the gymnasium amidst the clapping and the noise, after which General Haith proceeded to give a long-winded speech about what-it-means-to-be-a-member-of-the-Stoke-Ridge-community-and-how-it's-men-like-these-that-define-our-nation-et-cetera-et-cetera. Now you might be wondering how Slim got himself onto that stage, and though the details are unimportant—at least for now—the whole hoo-ha surrounding his return was mostly 'cause of his reputation as a formidable killing machine. See, when Slim started at Stoke Ridge he was a string bean cadet, a timid child without much physical promise: chicken legs and noodly arms and a vacuum-packed chest. Slim's mother, Wilhelmina Jenkins—we'll get to her—was a pothead who subsisted on reheated Hot Pockets, hardened Kraft mac n' cheese, and frozen mozzarella sticks. As a child, Slim always looked a bit sickly, always scrounging for food in the cupboards lest he be forced to reheat something moldy in the microwave, but by the time the second Bush decided to play his daddy's game, Slim had become the finest warrior Stoke Ridge had ever seen. Of course, Slim never knew his dad, but he must've benefited from some hunk's formidable genes. Though his hairline was receding by the time he was eighteen, his six-foot-five frame, accompanied by four years of bursting biceps and peck muscles filled out by four hundred push-ups a day, made the man quite a sight to behold. His newfound strength led to his award for bravery in Iraq during the First Battle of Fallujah—a hell of a fight for those boys in the red, white, and blue—for killing an entire platoon of alleged al-Qaeda operatives and taking a bullet straight through the jugular. And while the doctors said it was a miracle he'd survived, Slim said the real miracle was that they'd gotten him out before he could reload. He was a hero of sorts, but these days heroes are often shamed and quickly forgotten.

"And this man right here," General Haith said as he put his arm around Slim, "we'll never forget what he's done for us!"

"That's right," Slim continued. "Unlike some of us, I'm willing to fight! I don't just sit in my office all day watching kids do pushu—"

Dykes grabbed the mic. "Thank you for that Slim. How about another round of applause?"

While there were some grumblings in the audience about what Slim was talking about, the crowd cheered nonetheless 'cause that's what crowds do. Slim took back the podium. "I learned to fight once people started shooting at me. But as far as Stoke Ridge goes? Well, let's just say I didn't learn much at all . . . The thing is, it's not hard to develop fatherless kids into killers, and now we're the ones killing fathers across the world. Of course, a lot of these officers," Slim looked directly at Dykes, "don't have to do any killing at all, right? They only know about sending us boys out there while they sit behind simulators with whiskey and more viscous forms of lubrication. Some of 'em, like Dykes here, have never been to Iraq."

The audience fell silent, you could hear flies buzzing around the gym. Some kind of critter scampered across the aluminum roof. Slim sneered at Dykes, handed General Haith the mic, and stepped down from the stage. The general quelled the situation by bringing up freedom and the good fight and after a final round of hesitant applause, brown-fatigued cadets escorted the spectators onto the dessicated lawn, where sweet tea and lemonade were served in red plastic cups.

As for what happened next, there are only two people who know the story, and neither Slim nor Sgt. Dykes ever told me exactly. Whatever it was, it was violent and quick. Slim almost died. Here are the facts:

After hearing a commotion in Dykes' office, a group of cadets found Slim writhing on the floor, clutching his jugular, gurgling in agony. A crimson fountain spurted from the wound. The sergeant had tried to pop Slim's Adam's apple like bubble wrap, whispering the same phrase to himself over and over again: "Never listening. Never playing. Never so much as a goddamned hug. Never listening. Never playing. Never so much as a goddamned hug."

As soon as the cadets piled on top of Dykes, he began to thrash and kick around, breaking noses and shattering adolescent bones. Slim would've died if it hadn't been for

General Haith, who came in just in time to apply pressure to the wound. By the time Slim arrived at the hospital he'd lost over three pints of blood. He remained in a coma for three weeks and spent another month on morphine. General Haith, it must be said, was there every day to check on the young war hero and even though Slim was unconscious, the general stayed by his side just the same.

As for Dykes, after being treated for three cracked ribs and a pierced eardrum, he was released. Slim wouldn't file any charges 'cause this is the military we're talking about, but he did acquire a five-year restraining order, more than enough time, he thought, to get Dykes out of his life.

In later years, Slim told me putting Dykes in prison wasn't an option. There were no witnesses, technically. Slim's neck was already wounded, and the military is one of the best in the business when it comes to protecting its own during a scandal. Still, Dykes didn't get off easy. When he returned home, Stoke Ridge's former prom kings and defensive linemen were all waiting for him on his front lawn. After years of enduring Dykes' nasal voice, puppy dog eyes, and proclivity for whiskey and young cadets, the attack was the final straw for the Stoke Ridge community. Upon seeing the angry mob, Dykes snuck in the back door and spent the evening in a locked bathroom, drinking whiskey in the bathtub, and crying himself to sleep. The next morning, Dykes woke up to General Haith's voice on a loudspeaker: he had exactly one hour to get out of town. With his bags packed and nowhere to go, Dykes drove away in his rusty brown pickup, leaving only the second home he'd ever known.

On his way out of Stoke Ridge he passed three burning

effigies and a mob of angry townspeople. They threw full cups of sweet iced tea at his windshield and rolled old basketballs under his car. One man used a baseball bat to smash a side-mirror and another shot out his break lights with an assault rifle. As Dykes watched the Stoke Ridge church steeple fade in the rearview mirror, his car thumping forward, the back tire slowly losing air, he felt like vomiting and crying at the same time, which is exactly what he did at Exit 263.

For a time, Dykes lived as a vagrant, finding refuge in homeless shelters and the occasional motel, seeking company in old TV re-runs and cheap liquor.

2

Slim

Slim's scar was centered on his Adam's apple, white around the edges, the middle slightly pink. It took him months to be able to confidently look in the mirror, and even longer to be able to shave his neck. He went through speech therapy to recover his Southern drawl, but once the scar tissue healed and his voice came back—slightly gruffer now, more serious to match his eyes—Slim boarded a troop transport destined for a second tour in Iraq, with a clean-shaven head.

Being abroad, he later told me, somehow made him feel more connected, maybe 'cause he'd never known what it was to feel at-home. The second time around didn't inspire any heroism, and though his trigger-finger received the Distinguished Service Cross, Slim returned from that second tour a pariah in the media's eyes, blacklisted by the military for refusing to follow orders. What happened was, Slim had been up in a helicopter on a reconnaissance flight over Baghdad when he received an order to fire on a "terrorist" convoy. Now, Slim knew it was nothing more than a couple school buses 'cause he'd worked with one of them schoolteachers just the day before, but his commanding officer told him it was terrorists, goddammit, and if Slim knew what was good for him he'd blast 'em.

And so when some jackass behind a computer screen— Slim's words, not mine—said one of the terrorists was carrying a weapon, Slim just damn refused to fire, before watching in horror as the kids succumbed to an aerial drone. Fifty-six children died in the attack. It was enough for Slim to throw his dog tags out the helicopter right then and there. Slim quit.

After ridiculing and threatening to imprison the war hero, the brass decided to send him home lest he tell the truth about the school children they in fact killed by mistake. The commanding officers chalked it up to an alleged drug abuse problem with Slim that came to light after said faulty drone operation.

"Sometimes . . . well yes, I know about his *falsified* report," an army spokesperson said. "But he doesn't have his head screwed on just right. Have you seen his scar? Of cour—well of course it's tragic, Susan. I have kids too. But you know what Susan? Sometimes people make mistakes, and sometimes robots make mistakes."

Slim returned a veteran, disenfranchised, allegedly addicted to cocaine or heroine or crack. His tired face showed up in regional papers that blamed him for the fifty-six dead children, and the government was quick to discredit any stories he might tell otherwise. His mother had been addicted to weed (yes, it's possible) and the army used this to drive their point home: "High as a kite up in a helicopter, Slim was a loose cannon." One magazine spun it as: "CRACK, THE SILENT WAR: PORTRAIT OF A KILLER." Angry and alone, unable to confide in anyone about his experience, the twenty-year-old found solace for the summer in the North Carolina countryside, holed up in a Motel 6, livin' off of measly disability payouts and smoking weed under the cicada-filled pines.

A change soon came, as all changes do. Thanks to the GI Bill, a vestige of a different era, Slim enrolled at the University of North Carolina. He saved money for the fall by selling the mysterious baggies of drugs that kept showing up at his motel room to addicts passing through. He'd seen him once, a mysterious masked man who clumsily kept trying to frame Slim and cash-in on the headline. Slim saw the man stuffing dime bags through the crack under Slim's front door. Sometimes, if Slim left the bathroom window cracked, he'd come back to bags of drugs on the tile floor or in the toilet, so he started to put the seat down. It was the only way he was able to save some money, you see?

Slim kept to himself as much as he could, counting down the days until his new life could start. When he moved to UNC Chapel Hill, he wasn't so much forgotten as ignored: the conservative kids didn't trust him 'cause he'd spoken out against the war, and the liberals scoffed at his "heroism." Those who knew his past feared his neck scar, and those who didn't feared it more. At least, Slim told me, the rumors helped him focus on his studies, and though it remained a mystery to virtually all who knew him, Slim found refuge in the comforts of his own mind.

See, as a child he loved to read, even though the only two books he had growing up were his mom's two coffee-table books, *The Far Side* and *Calvin and Hobbes*. Finally at UNC he could really study what he wanted. "When everything's gone to shit," he once said, "there's nothing to pull you out of the hole like a bit of Jung or Rilke." Content with his books on philosophy and theory, Slim learned how to be alone, and even happy. And though he was paranoid for a time and had occasional nightmares about Sgt. Dykes, he didn't much care how drugs kept finding their way into his gym locker. He chalked it up to someone in the military brass trying to get him busted, but took advantage of the situation. He never did snort the stuff, but made a killing selling to frat boys and sorority girls who used it to study for the MCAT and LSAT and other acronymic exams. He only went to parties to sell off the drugs, which continued to appear throughout his sophomore year. He loved flirting with women but did fine without 'em just the same, and he couldn't have cared less about UNC's famous basketball team. After a near miss with campus police, Slim stopped selling to strangers and moved into his own place off Rosemary Street, a small white house with a brown roof and a leaky kitchen faucet that reminded him of his childhood home, for better or worse.

Finally able to look in the mirror without thinking of Sgt. Dykes, Slim finished his junior year on the dean's list, having spent all his time in the library trying to make sense of social theory. He had no real friends and preferred the solitude of his studies to the social platitudes; and though he would've liked to share his feelings with a friend or two, he didn't think anyone wanted to philosophize or discuss. Or maybe it was an excuse to avoid something deeper, 'cause despite his smooth talking, semi-heroic past, and laudable grades, Slim didn't believe he was much worthy of conversation. He kept his eyes on a future he couldn't quite envision. Paying his tuition only with the GI Bill money made things harder, but simpler. The truth was, a part of him wanted to be caught back when he was selling the mystery drugs. He felt like a phony—not like Holden Caulfield, but in an emptier way, he told me. And then one summer the thunderstorms began to roll in over the Piedmont, inviting Slim to read on the porch and listen to the rain, never once raising his head to notice the brown pickup parked down the street, concealed behind a willow tree, the driver slowly going insane.

3

Little Tyke

Dykes was a watcher. He never would have used the word stalk. Of course, Slim wasn't the only one Dykes kept an eye on—throughout the years there'd been other cadets, too—but Slim reminded Dykes of himself somehow, and so Slim remained at the top of the B.A.M. LIST.

In front of the computer screen, Dykes lived vicariously, fostering a connection to Slim that in reality he'd never known. Not that Slim had a Facebook—let's just say the government didn't allow it—but there were plenty of pictures from Slim's time in Iraq. While it didn't make Dykes happier to obsess over his cadets' digital lives until they blocked him, he still felt his online friendships were something profound; he spent most of his days on Facebook, forever connected, and forever alone.

Dykes was born sometime in 1976. His mother's name was Sasha and she didn't keep her maiden name. She was a sociable, voluptuous woman who liked shiny things and caviar and never ever slept alone. Dykes' father was named Trent and he sweated profusely. Short-tempered with a strong jaw but fatty face, and a receding hairline to boot. Trent never told Sasha he loved her, but he frequently slapped her ass.

"That's where I get it from," Dykes told me one night at my bar. "The sweating. My dad always had that film above his lip. He smelled like something sour, slightly rotten, something fierce. He liked things that looked expensive. That's why he married mother."

Chandler Dykes wiped his forehead with a thin paper bar-napkin. This was only the second time I'd ever spoken to him. "They only thought about themselves. And maybe that's what they saw in each other. What's the word, Lockart?"

"I don't know, Chandler. You're gonna need to give me more than that."

"It's a guy above a pond?"

"You mean Narcissus?"

"No, it's something else. But my mom spent her days down there, down by the pond. That's what I mean. Thinking about her art as she called it. I never understood it, to be honest. Seemed like something to pass the time. But my dad was always working. He stayed in his air-conditioned office. My mom always visited him at the end of the month. I only went in there once. It had mahogany doors and a red carpet, too. He had one of those desks with open leg space beneath it . . ."

Dykes' tone changed. He pulled at the tuft of his receding hairline. "Are you a family man, Lockart?"

"Why yes indeed, I am." I held up my left hand.

"Right, I'm so stupid. I'm sure she's beautiful."

"Yes, she is."

"You're a lucky man, Lockart. And a good husband, right?"

"Well I'd like to think so, yes. We all have our moments."

"You never ask her to do things, do you? You don't have a list of all the others, right?"

"All the others? On a list? Are we still talking about my wife?"

Dykes shuddered. "Lucky man, Lockart. A family man. Gosh. You know I had a nephew once?"

"I'm sorry to hear that."

"What? No he's still alive . . . I just haven't seen him in a while. It's been years now, actually. But here, I have a picture."

Dykes raised his buttocks off the barstool and pulled out an engorged wallet from his back pocket. "Here, take a look at him. That's him. He's cute, right?"

Dykes showed me a Polaroid of a teenage boy standing ankle-deep in a pool of water, holding up a fishing net full of live crawdads. The boy's eyes smiled but his mouth was unfazed. Something about his gaze made me feel pity.

"Such a good kid. Used to call me Uncle Chandler. Uncle Sarge."

"But not anymore?"

"He ran away from home, that's all."

Dykes went on to tell me how his parents drank heavily most nights. The excuse was catered parties, with caviar, of course. Being beautiful and/or rich was enough to suffice in Chapel Hill's community of nouveau riche, where it wasn't uncommon for middle-aged white people to be genuinely surprised that a waiter could also have a master's degree. Sasha and Trent were ignorant, blinded by the light from the chandelier's glare bouncing off fine jewelry and stiff Botoxed faces. They thought employing minorities for a catering service was both praiseworthy and progressive. In reality, most of their neighbors in the countryside were polite-but-not-kind types, hospitable wrinkled folk who owned confederate flag beach towels and believed statues should be forever.

They lived out in the country off old 86 near the town of Efland, where no two houses looked the same. It was—and still is, if I recall—a land of fields and meadows, tick-infested forests, and rusted dry creeks, where the landscape is landmarked by hay bales and cows, old tanks of propane out front dilapidated gas stations, a country where driving at night demands a strong pair of headlights and a discerning eye for suicidal deer. Out there it was easy to get lost—capture-the-flag, flashlight tag, and hide-and-seek were king—but Chandler Dykes knew none of this because he didn't have any friends growing up. Dogs barked at him, cats never rubbed up on his leg, and even though they hissed, Dykes was enamored with opossums. He never saw a cheerful bonfire, and the closest thing he had to a picnic was eating granola bars alone in the woods. He didn't know about hushpuppies or sweet tea or Cheerwine, and he could count on one hand the number of times he'd had chicken and dumplings. But according to tax forms, bank accounts, and grocery receipts, Chandler Dykes was a privileged child who grew up in a wooden house designed by a New York architect, a man who had a proclivity for bay windows, high ceilings, and eagle's nests. Light cascaded into the three-story mansion filled with glass tables, smooth objects, and expensive bowls from countries with names the neighbors couldn't pronounce. The Dykes family knew the price of everything but the value of nothing, like the cooking island in the custom kitchen, or the Swedish sauna in the west wing of the house.

Chandler slept in a lofted bedroom, ten feet above a cold, parquet floor. Sometimes, from on high, he watched geese and other birds pass by the bay windows, which were cleaned once a month by a man on a rope whose name was Jesus. Chandler's father hated immigrants but loved underpaying them: Mexican, Colombian, and Nicaraguan migrant workers tended the forty acres of property, trimming hedges, mowing grass, marking trees for destruction with pink tags. Sasha was kinder to the caretakers, occasionally saying "Hola señor" in her thick Southern accent, giggling in her polka-dot dress by the pond, flirting with the Central American boss she mistakenly called "Jeffy."

"I never really understood why she spent so much time down there by the water," Dykes recounted from the edge of his barstool, "wading around, setting up a camera on the far side. There was a structure there, made of wood. Kind of like a diving board? And she'd climb up and look down in the water, where she'd placed those oil containment booms, like the ones used for oil spills, filling the sections with different colored paint. Most of the time, she just stood at the top of the diving board, peering down toward that painted pond."

While Sasha contemplated her art, Trent threw catered parties. Chandler's early years were defined by buxom female waitresses serving boat-shoed Southern boys and diamond-studded women married to men who smoked cigars and drank bourbon. The women took champagne, hard lemonade, and mojitos and conversed about vacation homes and family pedigree. Never allowed to go downstairs in the evening, Chandler stayed upstairs and surveyed the garden parties from above, his father swaying from side to side, ogling the waitstaff and escorting them behind a shed next to the pond.

"It was always out behind the wood shed, on the far side of the pond. My mom knew, right? She must've known. But she just schmoozed with her artist friends and pretended not to notice. She was a concept artist, you know? Accepting reality wasn't really her thing. But I got used to sitting in my perch, staring down at their lives. There's something empowering about being above it all," he said, but the truth was Chandler Dykes wasn't above any of it, only that the height of his lonely loft instilled a sense of voyeuristic superiority in the young child.

The most egregious of their parenting errors was that they were never around. Instead, Dykes was more or less raised at the YMCA, which became his asylum. Since his father worked late and Sasha spent her days by the pond, both reasoned it would be easier to pay off the Y and not raise their son at all. So it went that Chandler spent his early days watching his peers—adolescent boys—exercising in the gym. One trainer named Tim taught him how to do push-ups, and another helped him with his biceps and said Chandler had nice arms. YMCA became Dykes' place of worship. He found a sense of home in the sweaty locker rooms, the humid chlorine air, and the sweet, sweet smell of freshly polished hardwood. He loved the deep inhales and the strained grunts, the suicides, the "drop give me twenties" and most of all, the squeaking sneakers on the court. And when his parents forgot to pick him up, he'd wait in the lobby by the weight room and watch the varsity boys workout. His favorite moment was when they finished and patted him on the head. *Little Chandler*, they called him, *Little Tyke*.

Dykes often reminisced about it all here at the bar, but it would always come back to the young cadet that got away. That summer of 2009, Dykes spent his days stalking Slim and his nights at the corner table, lamenting the past, wasting away on that damn Facebook and whiskey.

"My nephew, just look at him," Dykes showed me a Polaroid one drunken night. "What a good tyke. Did I tell you he used to call me Uncle Sarge? Can I take some peanuts home for Lenny?" His fingers were already in the bowl. "Lenny loves a late-night snack."

4

AKA The Beast

It's a shame college athletes didn't have a right to their own name back then. The all-American Hugh Dawton-Fields, aka The Beast, was no exception. One look at the young man and you'd be hard pressed to come up with a better nickname: seven-foot-two on his tippy-toes, size twenty-one shoe—the biggest in the NCAA—290 pounds after a full meal, hands the size of frying pans, and a wingspan of nearly eight feet. Standing under the ten-foot hoop, The Beast could touch the rim without even straining. He had bulging biceps, massive forearms, and a chest that often got in the way. He entered most thresholds sideways. One player described him as a seven-foot fridge, but as our man Slim would soon learn, appearances were deceiving when it came to The Beast.

Hugh Dawton-Fields's online identity was painted by secondary acquaintances, sports writers who thought they knew him, and fans who believed they understood why he played basketball and why he didn't like the spotlight. As a child, he was taunted for being tall, lanky, and quiet. When he hit puberty at thirteen, he was made fun of just the same. He was a dominant, forceful basketball player, but a frustrated one, too, not yet used to his staggering 6'8" frame. In high school, he had trouble controlling his strength, breaking more than a few noses and wrists along the way. On account of his clunky playing style, he usually fouled out by the end of the game. He didn't mind it though, watching from the sidelines. According to at least five NBA scouts, he had the size and talent but lacked the grit. Still, his averages spoke for themselves: 35.3 points, 21.5 rebounds, and 8.4 blocks, rarely playing more than half the game.

After a high school career that eclipsed even Wilt "The Stilt" Chamberlain's, The Beast entered UNC destined to become a legend. Professional scouts and well-dressed agents were baffled he didn't leave early for the NBA. In his first year in college, he won Player of the Year and as a sophomore he did it again. No one was able to crack The Beast's demeanor. Forever the quiet one who mistrusted the business side of things, Hugh Dawton-Fields vowed to finish his degree, a soft-spoken superstar who refused all interviews, always showed up to practice early, but left right on time just the same. He was old school, if that still meant anything, and while most believed he loved the college game because of the focus on team play, the truth was his main goal was a free education.

According to Sgt. Dykes, everything changed at the end of The Beast's junior year. He punched Assistant Coach Jim Brees right before March Madness and was suspended from the team. No one knows what Coach Brees said, but it most surely had to do with the death of The Beast's parents.

The punch came just weeks after the Dawton-Fields' family restaurant, Chez Nous, burned down. The most reliable story is that of Alex Morgan, a curly-haired point guard who spent quite a lot of time on the bench. "I won't tell you what was said because I know what you'll do with it, but trust me when I say what Brees said was unforgivable. Hugh came in with a big pasta casserole for us before practice. He was there to apologize for not playing in the tournament. He was just too broken up about his parents, poor guy. And then Coach Brees got in his face and started screaming to suck it up and be a man. It was brutal. That's when Hugh snapped."

Even if Alex Morgan's story is to be believed, verbal abuse was no excuse for detaching someone's retina. There were plenty of debates on ESPN and talk radio about what *could have been said* and if it even mattered, and if it did, *what did he say?* and if he did say it, *why?* Whatever the case, The Beast was suspended from the team and placed on academic probation, because it's one thing for the powers that be to pull strings for flagrant fouls or the occasional bloodied face, but nearly blinding a staff member? This was a serious offense that no PR expert or hoity-toity academic could right fix; but lest The Beast's college career end prematurely, the sentencing judge—an adamant basketball fan who had high hopes for UNC—saved Hugh Dawton-Fields from expulsion by allowing him and Coach Brees to settle out of court.

They simply couldn't afford to lose The Beast. They'd already spent three years selling FEAR THE BEAST T-shirts and had several brand sponsorships to maintain. In short, there were plenty of financial reasons to keep The

Beast at UNC, including financing the athletic director's sixtieth birthday party and re-designing the faculty lounges. He made the school millions, and if they could convince him to play again, UNC was still the favorite next season.

But until then, amidst the fumes of sizzling burger patties and golden-brown onions, Hugh Dawton-Fields was able to lose himself in the joy of cooking at The Skillet. The food truck was just off of Franklin Street, Chapel Hill's most famous thoroughfare lined with upscale fast-food joints, souvenir shops, and sky-blue merch boutiques. Although the grounds of UNC are known for their Southern charm—grassy knolls and oak trees, white-columned frat houses, and manicured sorority lawns—you don't have to walk far off of West Franklin to see another side of Chapel Hill.

The Skillet was permanently parked in a neighborhood which people like the Dykeses would refer to as the "rough part of town" beyond Rosemary Street. This was the implied area to avoid when "straying off campus" during freshman orientation, even if in truth it was safer than most fraternities. In earlier decades there'd been murders, of course, but which American town hasn't seen its share of bloodshed? And sure, there were rusted cars and even rustier bikes on dirt lawns, but there were also laughing kids playing in the street, vibrant community centers, tasty taquerias neighboring BBQ joints famed for their authentic cuisines, and crowded parks and basketball courts, all of this cordoned off by chain-linked fences to "protect" the precious grounds of UNC.

Here on Rosemary Street at the food truck that had no wheels, The Beast AKA Hugh Dawton-Fields made the best burger in the city, plain and simple. The truck had a low ceiling and a single light bulb that dangled from a string, which The Beast had to duck under each time he reached for more buns. When he turned to serve customers he had to watch out for his broad shoulders. Small red baskets with wax paper were stacked on the counter next to brown napkins. And though the golf scholarship students from Pinehurst and horseback riders from Southern Pines avoided The Skillet 'cause they were afraid of interacting with "poor" kids, the locals were thrilled to come down and catch a glimpse of the nation's most fearsome ballplayer serving up beef patties. High schoolers came in droves to play soccer or toss a football in front of The Skillet, hoping to catch a glimpse of the basketball phenom with a passion for cooking.

The Beast never served fries 'cause he believed they were cheap. Instead, he served home fries alongside caramelized onions and zucchinis and peppers both red and green. He sizzled grass-fed beef and free-range chickens and the occasional papaya or mango slice. There was a menu to order from 'cause most patrons weren't creative, but The Beast was adamant every time he greeted them: "If I've got the ingredients I can make it. What'll it be?" Compared to his brute force on the basketball court, The Beast had finesse behind the counter top—customers admired the way he kept an egg's yoke from running and how he stacked each ingredient so that nothing fell off when you took a bite.

Of course, the first time he met Slim, there was no such thing as Slim's Famous Burger, which you can order to this day from the chalkboard menu, though the writing is fading now and you really have to know the order by heart.

But I'm getting ahead of myself.

The day Slim and The Beast met in mid-June 2009, Slim approached The Skillet's window and planted both hands on the counter top. "Hey man, I'm trying to eat. You think you can help me?"

The skillet was sizzling. The Beast didn't hear him.

"Well you gonna turn around there, Wilt? See I was thinking of getting a hammmmburger—you think you can do that for me?"

The Beast didn't turn around immediately 'cause he assumed Slim was an annoying fan. He finished sautéing a few onions and then slowly turned to see who it could be.

"Yeah. Take a look at the menu." The Beast quickly returned to flipping a few patties, assuming Slim, like most of his customers, lacked imagination.

"Menu? What menu? Do I look like someone who doesn't know what he wants?"

"Glad to hear it." The Beast smiled. "Write down what you want on this slip of paper. You can check the boxes for the ingredients—"

"Now hold up, Wilt," Slim interrupted. He put his hand out, as if to calm him. "I ain't checking no boxes on no god-damn piece of paper. I don't mean to be rude, but I've got a system, see? Now here's what's gonna happen, Wilt—can I call you Wilt?"

"No. You can call me Hugh."

"Hugh. Wilt. Same difference. You're tall like Wilt Chamberlain. You probably play like him, too. But okay, I'll call you Hugh. You're that famous ballplayer right? Yeah I thought so. Good. Now what I want is some toma-toes. But not them cubes. I'm talking freshly cut circles. You think you can handle that for me?"

"You want cheese on that?"

"Well goddamnit Hugh, you think I'm finished? No sir, I'm just getting started. Now don't get behind Hugh—I know it's hard to think from way up there, but we got some work to do. I'm gonna need some lettuce on it and avocados, too. Double burger. And coleslaw—give me some of that spread on top. You getting this? Making us check boxes . . . what kind of place is this? So we've got lettuce and tomatoes and we've got coleslaw. We've got avocados. We've got two patties . . . you still with me? Good. Now I'm also gonna need a fried egg on that, with a slice of American cheese on top."

"No problem. Is that it?"

"Are you in a hurry, Hugh? You got a ballgame to get to or something? Don't worry about them behind me. The line can wait. This is summertime, Hugh. I'm just getting started. Now you best not be throwing it on there all random-like. I got a system, see? Lettuce, tomatoes, coleslaw, burger, cheese, avocados, burger, cheese, fried egg, bun. Except don't go putting that bun on top just yet—I gotta get my condiments on there too, understand? And make sure the egg ain't too runny, all right? I can't stand eating a soggy burger."

Slim watched closely as The Beast worked. "Those onions look mighty fine, yes indeed," he continued. "But I ain't going for that today—can't put onions on everything now can you? Now what condiments you got? I know you got ketchup, I can see it on your apron. And mustard it looks like, too. Is that Dijon? I bet it is. But I don't mess around with mustard. No sir. Not on a burger at least. Now here's the real question, Wilt the Stilt: you got any hot sauce my man?"

"All we have is Texas Pete . . ."

Slim slapped his leg like a real old-timer. "TEXAS MOTHER FUCKING PETE! Well goddamnit Hugh. You just made my day, you know that? It's the only hot sauce I can abide, and out of all the hot sauces in the whole wide world, you've only got Texas motherfucking Pete! We may just end up being friends after all." He stuck out his knuckles to pound fists. The Beast reciprocated.

"Now I'm gonna be back here quite often this summer," Slim said, "so you better get used to making Slim's Burger. I like this place, it makes me feel at ease. I don't cook too often and let's just say this is kind of *my area.* Now why in the hell is this place called The Skillet? Isn't that a griddle you're cooking on? Is your boss illiterate? No disrespect, Hugh, but words gotta have meaning."

After Slim finished eating, he stayed a while at the window to watch The Beast cook. The two hardly spoke but seemed at ease with each other's presence—at least this is what Sgt. Dykes surmised from across the street in his pickup. From behind a pair of binoculars, Dykes wondered how any two men could be so comfortable with each other, and so quickly.

5

Enter, Chandler Dykes

I knew he'd be trouble by the way he approached, striding up to the bar as if he owned the place.

"Hello. My name is Sergeant Chandler Dykes. But you can call me Dykes. That's what my friends call me."

His body odor was fierce.

"I bet you're Lockart. That's your name on the sign, right? Got the place for cheap I bet. That's what I did with my cabin, just out back in the woods. You can see it from your backyard if you squint through the trees. Well, nice to meet you neighbor!"

There are few things more telling than a weak handshake. He had a terse mouth, squirrelly eyes, and awkward posture, too, and although his shoulders were tense, his arms hung limp at his sides. My wife, Jane, refused to be anywhere near him. Those first weeks he was preoccupied, hunched over his laptop at the table in the corner, the one beneath the framed print of Edward Hopper's *Nighthawks*.

He'd sit there in front of his black PC computer—one of those old bulky things with a squishy red pimple in the middle of the keyboard—and take advantage of the free Internet, listening to lord knows what on an outdated MP3 player with those headphones that curl around the back of the ear.

After three weeks of mostly drunken silence, save the slapping on the keyboard and the occasional grunt or moan, Dykes started sitting with his computer at the bar. Sometimes he'd flip the screen around to show me god-awful CNN headlines, inane Facebook posts, and the like. Thankfully the computer would eventually overheat, and that's when he started to tell me his life story—like a lonely geriatric, who thinks their past is more real than their waking life. His complaint-filled soliloquies were laced with inconsequential anecdotes and half-truths, but what I remember most is the first time he asked about Slim and The Beast.

He had on a ketchup-stained shirt that night and a foul stench on his breath. His right hand looked burned and he smelled like a camp fire.

"Just got back from Stoke Ridge," Dykes said. "Saw an old friend. Did some house work with him."

"Is that right? Well I've got this door hinge I'd like—"

"Oh, it's a sad town now. Good memories, though. They can take everything else . . . but they can't take memories, can they! Hey, Lockart . . ." Dykes surveyed his burnt hand. "Can you give me a damp rag? Damn matches. Should've used a lighter, almost let him get away . . . say, you ever heard of this basketball player they call The Beast?

Apparently he's a big deal—best player at UNC."

"Maybe you should look his real name up."

Dykes grabbed at his backpack and pulled out his computer. "I already have. It's all bullshit. Just anecdotes. See?"

He shoved the laptop onto the bar.

"Here, look at this. See? Nothing special. Just stats and facts, that's all."

"There's got to be more than this, right? I mean, this is the Internet—you can find everything on here! I mean, why is there so little about his parents dying in their kitchen?"

"You know how I feel about that laptop on my bar, Chandler. Take it back to your table in the corner. You can plug it in next to the jukebox. You know I don't abide gadgets around libations."

"Don't worry. It's protected. I mean I can protect it. It's fine. I'll go to my table. That's where I belong, right?"

He punched away at the keyboard with two index fingers, cursing my slow Wi-Fi, drinking enough whiskey to put most men in a ditch.

"I can't find anything about him!" He said one winter's day. "Nothing at all! It's all boring sports stuff. Who is this faggot anyway? What is he hiding?"

"I've already told you not to use that word in my bar, Chandler. I won't ask again."

"I mean, there's gotta be something more about him . . . I know there's more. There has to be. Why does Slim like him? There's more. There's gotta be something. . ."

"It's like Jane said: there's much more to a person than what's on the Internet."

"What do you mean?"

"Well, using the Internet to learn about a person is like . . . it's like going to Applebee's for a steak."

"But I love Applebee's."

"That's fine. Lot's of people do. The point is, what you're getting isn't the real thing."

"What do you mean the real thing? It's real. It's steak."

"It's frozen. It's industrial. It's not natural, that's all."

"But I go there after Denny's. Grand Slam at Denny's and then Applebee's for a drink."

I chose not to say anything.

"Ah, here we go. This about sums it up, Lockart. Listen to this, here it is: Hugh Dawton-Fields was projected to be the number one pick in the NBA Draft until he knocked out UNC Assistant Coach Jim Brees. Although it was a year ago, many analysts believe it will affect his draft position."

Dykes took refuge in inventing his own image of The Beast in the blue screen. This wasn't anything new. He was reading from Wikipedia again: 1. High School; 2. College; 3. Family Tragedy and Coach Jim Brees. Dozens of blogs and sports websites highlighted The Beast's supposed aggression, sparking debates over how safe he was for the family-friendly NBA, if new rules should be made, if Jim Brees deserved it and why, and what the limits of violence in sports were, et cetera et cetera. All of the analysts speculated, which is all they could do 'cause The Beast never agreed to speak, but I had no input.

"Like I've said before, when it comes to people, I rely on conversation for information."

"He's dangerous. He should be banned. What if he

hurts him?"

"Hurts who?"

"Never mind. His parents died in a fire . . . you know it's almost impossible for an arsonist to get caught? Forty-eight hours. That's all."

I didn't care for specifics. "*Enough*, Chandler. And you can't be staying as late as you did last night. Last call."

Like a child, Dykes pretended not to hear me and continued jabbing at the keyboard. "Just a couple more seconds. You're going to like this. Trust me."

"Chandler, please. I've got to close up. My wife's waiting for me."

"They're making a documentary about him. His life story. You know about Jim Brees? There's a preview on ESPN tomorrow. Too bad you don't have a TV in here. Maybe we can get it streaming? I'll come in early so we can see . . . See you in the a.m." Dykes gathered his things.

"You're not coming in early, Chandler. I won't be here."

"Geez, okay. I'm leaving. Can I have some peanuts for Larry?"

"Not tonight, Chandler. I'm all out."

For some reason that night, I decided to watch him walk all the way back to his cabin, high stepping and stomping, stumbling over brambles, swinging his keys around his index finger until he fell to the ground. The keys must have fallen somewhere on the forest floor because after a few minutes of drunken stumbling, Dykes pulled out his computer and got down on both knees, using the laptop's blue glow to sift through small twigs and dead leaves.

6

Tar Heels

Slim and The Beast's friendship blossomed that summer. For the first time since Stoke Ridge, Slim had something resembling brotherhood, and for the first time since his parents had died, Hugh had something resembling family. Although it felt like their pasts were finally behind them, what they didn't know was Dykes was watching all of it unfold from the rear view mirror of his pickup. Hugh even unknowingly cooked Slim's Famous Burger for Sgt. Dykes one afternoon, when Slim wasn't there, of course; Dykes made a point to mention if Hugh wanted to taste a *real burger*, he should come out to a place called Lockart's Bar, which he added to his growing list of locally owned spots to try out.

Towards the end of that otherwise peaceful summer, The Beast received a letter from UNC outlining his future:

August 15, 2009

Dear Mr. Dawton-Fields:

After careful deliberation and discussion with Mr. Jim Brees, the administration has agreed to reinstate you on the Varsity Basketball Team. If you choose to return to the team, you must publicly apologize, on camera, to the University of North Carolina and to Mr. Brees.

If you do not intend to return, you will be expelled from the University of North Carolina, effective immediately. Furthermore, Mr. Brees will pursue criminal charges as well as further monetary compensation for physical and psychological injuries sustained.

Please inform of us of your decision by the end of this week.

Sincerely,
Chase L. DuBois, Esq., Athletic Director
The University of North Carolina

With The Beast suspended and thus facing a major decline in ticket sales, TV ratings, and merchandising, UNC was desperate to reinstate their breadwinner. Though Hugh knew he had more bargaining power than the letter stipulated, back then, as a student athlete, he was in no real position to stand up to the mighty pen-wielders. And while he hated the thought of sitting next to Coach Brees, he wanted a degree. He agreed to the reinstatement conditions and followed the proviso to a T, getting Slim to take a picture of him holding up a note card that said: "I'm Sorry, University of North Carolina and Mr. Jim Brees." He opened a Twitter account (@TheRemorsefulBeast) and posted the photo for everyone to see. Coach Brees and UNC's lawyers were peeved, but accepted the tweeted apology nonetheless.

A SLAM Magazine article entitled "The Return of

The Beast" made it official. Thousands of Carolina blue "Return of The Beast" and "Fear The Beast" T-shirts covered the backs of giddy kids moving into the dorms. Plastic cups held in storage boxes were returned to Dean Dome vendors; baseball caps and wall posters were back-ordered immediately.

In addition to all the money pouring into UNC, marketing executives at video game companies, fast-food restaurants, and sports stores began to brainstorm how exactly to sell The Beast once he made it to the NBA. The draft was fast approaching—June 2010—and the faster they could woo The Beast with promises of untold riches, the better their fiscal projections for the following year. But Hugh never accepted gifts and, as usual, refused to speak with the media. The less he spoke about basketball, the bigger his legend became. As new students moved into the dorms, lugging cheap AC units up concrete stairs, East and West Franklin Street began teeming with chatter. *This* was the year UNC would win the ACC Championship; *this* was the year the Duke Blue Devils, their nemesis, would fall. The analysts analyzed, the pundits opined, opponents devised game plans, and fans prepared vicious chants. . .but Hugh didn't falter under the pressure.

Slim and Hugh moved into a one-story house in Davie Circle, just off East Franklin Street. Slim had been living down in Carrboro, but his one-bedroom place wasn't big enough for two man-children. The house—raised on stilts 'cause it used to flood during hurricane season—was in a modest neighborhood of one-story homes, a short walk away from the Sunrise Biscuit Kitchen, that steamy one-room restaurant serving the best homemade buttermilk biscuits

North Carolina has to offer (scrambled egg, Tabasco-spiced sausage, and melted cheddar cheese). Though they only lived in Davie Circle from August 2009 until June 2010, it might as well have been an entire childhood for all the joy and growth involved.

They ate oatmeal with bananas and brown sugar in the morning. They argued like brothers about doing the dishes 'cause Slim never cleaned as he cooked. They scheduled the same times for class so they could walk together up to campus, eating lunch at the same time and going out for giant burritos at Cosmic Cantina, that once-rustic Mexican restaurant with a nondescript decor, fresh ingredients, and burritos bigger than most faces.

Back at home, sated, two philosophized and played video games and drank whiskey and occasionally, Slim smoked weed. While Slim studied philosophy, The Beast tried to recall old family recipes, since most of the family cookbooks were lost in the fire he was determined to preserve his parents' memory. Both found Greek life pathetic and preferred hosting intimate house parties. Even though Hugh was popular, they kept to themselves most of senior year, often foregoing late nights on Franklin Street to watch Seinfeld reruns and sports documentaries, arriving early at Elmo's Diner where they preferred tables to booths on account of the leg space.

There was a bond there, you could see it. They were like brothers. See, Hugh couldn't go anywhere without being asked to sign his nickname, and some students still berated Slim for his time in Iraq, but when they were together, people let them be. Able to sit in the same room for hours in silence—solidarity in solitude, as Slim called it—Slim and Hugh stopped worrying about what others thought and began to question what they thought about themselves. Slim and Hugh chose serenity over popularity, blocking out everything, including the purr of a rusty brown pickup idling down the street.

March Madness loomed heavy. NBA scouts flocked to the Dean Dome in hopes of wooing their biggest prospect, even if there was some doubt about his "talent ceiling." He was a top prospect because of his size rather than a true passion for the game. He began showing up late for morning practices 'cause he'd been down at the local market buying the freshest ingredients, and twice in February he almost missed tip-off for a home game to cover a friend's shift down at The Skillet.

Now sure, The Beast had a beautiful hook shot and could post-up any man in the country, but for the life of him he couldn't make it down the court in less than ten seconds. According to a video analysis Dykes played for me at the bar, "his defense won't cut it in the NBA. He'll have to come out to the three-point line and get around picks. In his first three years backpedaling on fast breaks, The Beast broke fifteen noses, four wrists, and one player's hand."

The Beast was a force to be reckoned with, even at the next level of the game. "He may be a ruthless specimen of pure muscle that doesn't play defense," a Boston Celtic said, "but his intimidation factor is undeniable. Bottom line? I know some players who'd refuse to face him. He's the most exciting and terrifying player I've ever seen."

Another scout from the Chicago Bulls: "That man is something special. Good for the NBA? I don't know. But he sure is a specimen. He's smart. You see his GPA? The passion will come. He's still young. He's already an All-Star on the stat sheet." Not everyone, however, was so enthralled. "You mean Dawton-Fields?" An anonymous Spurs player remarked. "He's a lunatic. Plain and simple. I can only speak for myself, but I don't want him in the league. This isn't a boxing ring. Fundamentals are important. And I'll say it right now: if he's on the court, I'm not playing. It's not worth it for me. I'm too old for that. I've already won championships. I don't need to get bruised up playing against a guy like him. I don't play that kind of basketball . . . leave it in the streets." A high school teammate-turned-NBA-referee also warned: "Hell no, I never played against him . . . not even in practice. Why? 'Cause he's dangerous. Is letting a wolf into a dog park a good idea? Is releasing a giant hawk above a preschool your idea of fun?"

Whichever way you looked at it, The Beast was a lottery-pick. In a draft that was lacking, he was guaranteed to bring in money. Despite limited minutes (about twenty-five per game) The Beast averaged twenty-seven points and thirteen rebounds per game, sweeping through most teams with terrifying force, and March 14, 2010, provided a fitting end to the regular season. Following UNC's dominating run through the ACC, the stage was set for the greatest rivalry in competitive sports, two shades of blue that make all the difference: Duke vs. UNC, the Battle of The Blue Bloods on Tobacco Road. Nine miles makes all the difference down Highway 15-501. The stage was set for the 2010 ACC Tournament Final, remembered as one of the greatest and most stomach-turning examples of competition ever seen on a basketball court.

The game started out normally enough. Duke was

shooting lights out from three, picking apart UNC's 3-2 zone defense. The Beast made up for it though, garnering fifteen points, ten rebounds, seven blocks, and only two fouls by the end of the first half. Halfway through the second half it was clear neither team was giving in: The Beast was playing his smartest game since the beginning of the season, avoiding foul trouble by blocking shooters' views with his pan hands, yet Duke was still shooting a season-high 55 percent from three. As Duke continued light it up from behind the arc, UNC's elderly fans could only shake their bejeweled heads in vain. But then, with eight minutes left, UNC made a furious comeback, going on a 25-10 run to all but secure the ACC championship. With one minute to go, UNC was up by eleven. Everyone except Duke fans thought the game was sealed.

The band section in the Dean Dome started playing, "We Are The Champions." More than a few Carolina fans left the stadium to beat the 15-501 traffic. But then a hush fell over the thinning crowd as Duke connected on a barrage of three-pointers, cutting the lead from eleven points to five in a matter of seconds. After UNC missed a crucial free throw, Duke ran up the court and didn't hesitate to hit another three. Now UNC was only up by two. They took the ball out under their own basket, at the far end of the court. The cheerleaders couldn't help but cheer nervously. Hoping for a turnover and another missed free throw, Duke called on a bench warmer by the name of Michael Jinson to put The Beast, UNC's worst free-throw shooter, on the foul line.

Here's the thing: Michael "Jincy" Jinson never should've been on the basketball court. He was a six-foot-one freshman with a mop of floppy hair. Before March 14, 2010, he'd never so much as said hello to a man over seven feet. Although "Jincy" was a great defender, willing to sacrifice his body for the play, he was nothing more than the prototypical Duke bench warmer, out there to scrap, follow orders, and take a charge. So when one of Jinson's teammates sarcastically said, "You won't be able to take a charge on The Beast. The only way to get him ejected is to get your finger up his ass," well, the young go-getter took it literally, considering it his duty to sacrifice his index finger for the game. And so he shuffled out into the spotlight, a ceremonial sacrifice, a tactic The Beast had seen plenty of times.

The Beast inbounded the ball to try and stay out of the play altogether. UNC's point guard tripped and bonked the ball straight back to him. By the time The Beast reached down, Jincy's finger was already on its way. Only one cameraman caught it. Everyone else focused on the ball. Michael Jinson screeched and wailed on the floor. The audience gasped. There was a collective scream. Sucking in air, chest heaving up and down, Jinson whimpered like a child as he clutched his right hand, a twisted claw gushing blood onto the court. *The New York Times* called it "one of the most grotesque injuries seen in sports." At least one UNC fan vomited into a 64-ounce cup. The Beast, in a rage, was held back until the replay confirmed everyone's suspicions. Sure, Jinson's hand had gone up The Beast's shorts, but did this warrant The Beast pulverizing five fingers? After the nauseated ball boys mopped up the last of the blood, Duke made two free throws and gained possession to ultimately win the game on a buzzer-beater, though no one would remember the score.

The Foul Heard Around the World ended The Beast's college career. In the months leading up to the NBA Draft, basketball fans remained split on The Beast's antics. On the one hand, they were terrified of what he'd do next, but on the other hand, this was part of why they watched sports. "Wait 'til he gets here," an anonymous OKC Thunder player said, "We'll show him what a hard foul really means. No, I'm not scared of him. Of course not! He won't score a single basket. You can quote me on that." In the words of a radio host: "Well yes, of course Larry, you're right. He can be brutish at times. But I saw the replay. Do you know why he attacked that kid Jinson? These kids are still kids. You've got to remember that. Do you know about his past? Tragic story, really." Whatever the opinion (and there were plenty) The Beast was still a guaranteed top-ten pick.

In June 2010, he and Slim packed the car, a rickety '93 Jeep Cherokee with a massive stick shift and a pair of furry red dice dangling from the rear-view mirror for good luck. The windshield wipers had no lubrication and screeched back and forth spreading dead bugs in an arc across their view. The passenger side-mirror was broken, too, and if either of their mothers had been alive, they would've made a comment about the lack of airbags. The seat belts were also useless 'cause they had no stopping mechanism: if they got into an accident, they'd both be ejected—the car was flat-out dangerous, but neither of them thought twice as they drove away from a coming summer storm.

It was raining when they left, and you may not know it if you aren't from around here, but summertime means summer storms, and not just thunderstorms, but proper hurricanes, and in June 2010, Hurricane Beverly was welcoming in the season, one of the earliest category fives in history, churning somewhere off the coast, picking up water and speed. The meteorologists said it'd make landfall that very night, but they weren't too worried about it on account of they were headed westward—they just had one quick stop to make off Exit 263, to taste a burger at a bar named Lockart's. And that's where I come in.

7

Enter, Slim & The Beast

Lockart's was nestled in a clearing at the forest's edge, surrounded by tall pines on a hill above Old Hope Creek. Wind chimes hung from two small oak trees in the back-yard. An abstract, metallic sculpture reflected the sunlight, designed and built by the famed sculpture artist known as H.G. Jane, who also happens to be my wife. There was a stairway out back—steep wooden steps with sizable gaps between 'em—leading up to a small bedroom where I sometimes slept. The roof was slanted and the carpet was white, and I slept on a futon next to a small blue light. As for the bar, well, there wasn't much inside, but just 'cause something's spartan doesn't mean it's empty.

The jingling of the bell and creaking of the screen door revealed a shotgun-style tavern of modest acclaim whose three rectangular windows beckoned in the eastern sun. There were three booths next to the windows—thick wooden tables, dark oak with a waxy finish, which Dykes liked to scrape at with his unkempt fingernails—but most people sat at the bar 'cause Lockart's wasn't a restaurant at the time. In the back right corner was a that framed print of *Nighthawks* I've mentioned, just above the Dykes' favorite table.

The dark oak bar ran half the length of the tavern, with a hatch at the far end that was heavy to lift. Tall stools lined up in front of the bar, high enough so short legs couldn't reach the floor. The whole place smelled like incense—Nag Champa, to be precise—'cause neither Jane nor I like the smell of beer-stained floors and Clorox. Who does?

Did I mention the screen door was rusty? The hinges creaked when the big one came in, accompanied by a heavy, humid breeze and a buzzing mosquito. The bell above the door jingled again as his slightly smaller companion blasted through the screen door, knocking loose a hinge that fell to the ground and rolled across the floor of the otherwise empty bar. He didn't notice.

"One whiskey, a sweet tea, and two burgers—quick!" They were in a rush, he said, The Beast was headed to the NBA.

I knew who my first customers of the day were immediately.

"Excuse me," Slim repeated. "Anyone here? *I said I'll have a whiskey.* And my man over here will have an iced tea. What kind of a business is this? Maybe they're in the kitchen . . ."

Slim stood up, leaning over the bar. "Now listen up, whoever's back there. I know you're there 'cause the door ain't closed. You know who this man is? They call him The Beast."

"They're probably just in the bathroom, Slim," The

Beast said without a hint of irritation.

"Someone's messing with us, Hugh. I can feel it."

I let out a smoke-filled sigh from the back corner table where I'd been watching. "No use getting antsy, mister," I said. "I'm the owner, see? And I don't serve liquor until three. That's just policy. It isn't anything against you boys, but you'll have to wait for that whiskey. " I walked over to the two of 'em. "The name's Lockart. Welcome to my bar."

Sunlight shimmered through the smoke and dander floating through the air. The Beast squinted and held out his hand. "Excuse us sir, nice to meet you. Do you think we could have a drink? We're not staying long, what with the hurricane. Just a quick pit stop, that's all. Trying to beat the traffic."

I shook his hand. The Beast continued: "We don't want any trouble, just a drink and a burger, if possible. We've heard a lot about it—one of the best in the area, so we're told. And a whiskey and a lemonade."

"Sweet tea."

"What?"

"Sweet tea," I said. "Your friend there asked for a whiskey and a sweet tea, unless I'm mistaken?"

"You got a problem with that?" Slim threatened with a juvenile aggression. I recognized him from Chandler's Polaroid.

"Well," I took a long drag from my cigarette and went around the bar. "I guess I do, don't I? Like I said before, I don't serve alcohol until three. Now, I'd be more than happy to get you some sweet tea or lemonade, but as for the burgers, well this is a bar, we ain't known for our burgers.

And as for the whiskey? I'm sorry, not until the clock hits three. Now I don't know if you noticed when you first came in, Slim—"

"How the hell do you know my name?"

"I pay attention. Your friend here said it about fifteen seconds ago. As for you," I looked at Hugh, "They call you The Beast?"

"People call me that—"

"He's famous," Slim interrupted. "You watch UNC basketball?"

"Can't say I do. I stopped a while back, but I don't need a TV to know who he is. Now as I was saying, Slim, I don't know if you noticed when you first came in, but you dislodged a door hinge and now it's on the floor." I pointed down. "I just spent the morning down on my knees trying to fix it. But apparently I didn't do too good a job. My wife, Jane, does the real work around here . . . she's a whiz with that kind of stuff. Screws and hinges aren't my specialty. For the life of me I can't figure them out. Did you see the sculptures out front? Jane made those, too. She said I needed to add some panache to the place. Now you mentioned you're in a hurry, but you can't outrun a hurricane. As for your nickname, The Beast, well, I've heard of you plenty."

"What's that supposed to mean?"

"This really *is* something. I mean what are the odds? Here you are, The Beast of legend, standing in my bar. You know you're driving straight into a storm, don't you?"

"We're not driving into it, we're getting away from it," Slim replied.

"Not tonight you aren't," I chuckled. "All this technology

and you forget to use your eyes. You don't need a satellite to tell you the whole interstate is clogged. The storm's a comin'. No use trying to escape it. But this is interesting, take a seat. It's almost whiskey time."

"We're thirsty now, mister," Slim said.

"Well lets start you with sweet tea."

Slim looked at The Beast. The Beast looked at his watch. "I think we need to get going. Like you said, there's traffic to beat."

"Ha," I smiled. "Sometimes you beat the traffic, and sometimes the traffic beats you. . . Do me the courtesy and wait a couple minutes. I haven't had a customer all day."

Slim and The Beast shifted in their seats, exchanging those looks young people give each other when they're trying to get away, formulating an escape plan as an elder starts to ramble.

I placed two tall glasses of sweet iced tea on the bar, complete with lemon slices and plenty of ice. "You want to leave, I get it. Okay, that's fine. But at least wait for me to serve you one glass of whiskey. I've got something y'all need to hear."

The Beast was polite. "One whiskey, all right. We can wait for one drink, Slim. Why the three o'clock rule, mister?"

"Call me Lockart. I used to have what some might call a drinking problem, and nothing good comes from getting started before lunch. Everyone needs limits, no matter how far gone. Now, it's not like I'm scrambling for the stuff when the clock hits three. Sometimes I'll go for days before drinking again. But the *point* is setting limits. Understand?

This Chandler character who keeps coming in could learn a thing or two about that . . ."

Slim choked on his sweet tea. "What'd you call him?"

"Dykes. Chandler Dykes. Though he likes people to call him Sergeant. The bozo's been coming in here for a while now. He just goes on and on, and most of the time, it's about you two."

"Hugh, let's get out of here. *Now*." Slim made for the door, but stopped at the threshold. "You said he lives around here?"

"Yes indeed, just out back behind the bar in that rickety old cabin . . ."

"Hugh, let's go. I'll tell you in the car."

"Good luck finding a room in a motel tonight," I said. "You think you two are the only ones trying to get out of town? There are tens of thousands of people heading west. I-40 is jammed. This storm isn't messing around. Beverly's the real deal. Plus, Chandler knows you're going to Milwaukee, he's been talking about it all week. He's either waiting for you there, or he's hunkered down under the covers in his cabin."

"Slim, what the hell is this guy talking about?"

Slim lowered his head and returned to the bar. "I'm gonna need that whiskey now. Hugh, there's a lot to explain."

On the hour, I poured us three whiskeys.

"So," Slim said. "What's he been saying, Lockart?"

"Well, a lot of things," I replied. "More than I care to recount, in fact. He's either at that table in the corner with his laptop looking up your friend here, or he's sitting right where you're sitting, lamenting one thing or another. Mostly he talks about his past, his childhood. And about you, Slim. Calls you his nephew. As for you, Hugh, he can't seem to figure you out. It drives him crazy.."

"Figure *me* out? Why me?"

Slim's anger returned. "Fuck this, Hugh. Let's hit the road. We can make it to Greensboro before the worst of it, even if it takes a couple of hours in traffic. Lockart, you won't tell him we were here, right?"

"I know he's a nut—"

"You have no idea."

"Look," I replied. "I won't let Dykes do anything to you. He respects me, and I've got information you need to know. The more you know about him, the easier it'll be to confront him—whether that's here in my bar or in a parking lot in Milwaukee, at least here I can protect you."

Slim walked over to the open screen door again. "Talk about shitty luck. I really thought he was out of my life for good."

"In truth, I think he's just as afraid of running into you, Slim."

My words reminded Slim of something. A gust of wind made the chimes on the front-porch sing. The edge of the storm rumbled over the pines.

"Alright, Lockart, but I'm gonna need another," Slim sat back down and swigged his whiskey. "Where do we begin?"

8

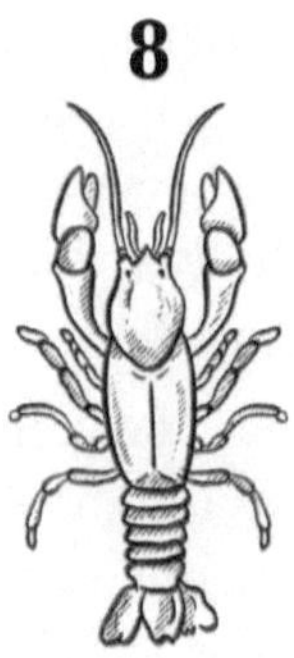

Crawdads & Lawn Mowers

Slim was born in an elevated trailer atop a hill above a creek that runs under the James Taylor Bridge. The place smelled like Hot Pockets, wet laundry, and mold, and the crawlspace beneath the trailer smelled like somewhere rodents go to die. The house was a tube small enough to tow with a pickup, a flimsy metallic structure whose innards were made of crackling drywall and asbestos. There was a master bedroom—his mother's—a hallway, living room/ kitchen, bathroom, short hallway, then Slim's bedroom, which only fit a single bed. Insulation foam crept out of the plaster walls throughout the year, doing little to keep the air in or out. The roof leaked constantly, as did the kitchen sink, whose drip-drip-dripping kept Slim up at night. Whenever he had the courage—he was afraid of the dark as a kid— he'd tiptoe out of his room, down the hallway, and into the living room/kitchen, where his feet would sink into the sodden brown carpet. He'd squish back through the kitchen on his tiptoes and crawl into bed. The dark brown walls in his bedroom absorbed most of his trusty nightlight's blue glow. The rest of the trailer was filled with exposed, swinging light bulbs whose fuses were almost always at their end. Sometimes his mother slept in her bedroom, but usually she piled damp laundry on top of her bed and got high in the living room/kitchen, where she often passed out.

The trailer trembled during hurricane season and should've been destroyed during Hurricane Fran. When the summer storms flooded the nearby creak, Slim would sit on the makeshift porch and watch the water rush beneath the trailer, carrying debris to the low point down the hill. In the Trees showered pine needles in the fall, and icicles slapped the aluminum roofing in the winter. In the springtime, when the trees burst yellow, pollen and dander coated the trailer. Slim had his fair share of allergies—cats, pollen, dust, and the like—and thanks to his mother's cat Eddy, who shat in a box in the house, Slim learned to live with pungent smells and itchy, watery eyes. He got used to the discomfort and the loneliness, too, all of it exacerbated by his mother's marijuana addiction.

The dank exhalations of Wilhelmina Jenkins fogged Slim's first impression of this here world. She was a single mother with a mole on her chin that sprung a singular coarse hair that never met a pair of tweezers in its lifetime. Her long brown hair reached to her calves and her petite body could tolerate ungodly amounts of weed. Her favorite activity, regardless of season, was to mow the brown lawn with a joint in her mouth, kicking up dirt and small rocks with an outdated lawn mower that didn't have a blade protector and made an antiquated sound. She spent her summers in the yard, the mower's blare blocking everything else out. Long story short, Wilhelmina despised her parents and she was pretty sure they despised her, too. After her father died of a heart attack from mixing uppers and booze, her mother moved to Miami and abandoned her eighteen-year-old pregnant daughter with nothing more than a tube-like trailer next to a creek. By the time Slim came screeching out into the world, any inkling of Wilhelmina's maternal instincts had seeped into the abused couch, down in the crevices among the remnants, where worn pennies and weed stems competed with Dorito dust for dominion. Wilhelmina only hugged Slim when she wanted to cuddle, so Slim spent most of his infancy sitting on the soggy carpet building Lincoln Log towers and swallowing more than a few imitation brand Legos. In the warm months, Slim spent as much time as he could outside, alone with his thoughts in the ankle-deep waters of James Taylor Creek.

Slim loved searching for crawdads. He'd poke at the mud with a stick and splash around in hopes of uncovering the evasive creatures, his jeans rolled up, his voice ready to yelp at the first ripple. He'd stand there for hours, waving off Wilhemina's calls for supper, and when he got hungry enough, he'd trudge up the hill in dirty brown socks, which his mother never bothered him to take off once inside.

"Whenever I got home, dinner was usually half-eaten," Slim slipped his whiskey. "Hot Pocket leftovers on the kitchen table with my mom passed out on the couch. I didn't like being at home, but school wasn't much better. Momma's second favorite activity—after mowing the lawn high—was hotboxing to-and-from school. I tried to stick my head out the window but it didn't always work. I wanted to learn but I was put in the special-ed class 'cause I was usually too damn high. Some quack prescribed me Adderall, which made me pissed off, you know?"

Slim paused to bite his thumbnail, going at it from the edge. "Couldn't make any friends. So by the time I was on fifty milligrams a day, always nauseated, missing class to use the bathroom every twenty minutes, it defeated the purpose of being on the drug in the first place. Forget about thriving. I was terrible at science and math. My test scores were terrible, which was all they ever cared about."

Slim pulled his thumbnail from his mouth and placed it on the bar napkin. "I liked to talk things out, but no one ever listened. By high school, I was a bonafide drop-out. I was always down by the creek. And then one day I went far downstream, and that's when I saw them through a clearing. All of 'em had nets. And there he was, this big, impressive man snapping pictures and giving 'em high fives."

Slim's face lit up. "I'd never seen anything like it. He was like a savior. He was everything I wasn't—tall and strong and confident, with all his cadets laughing in the creek, picking up buckets full of crawdads, playing with each other like kids are supposed to, right? All those years looking for crawdads and I was just in the wrong part of the creek. I saw my tribe that day—a different tribe, in any case. It was the first time I'd ever witnessed a community I wanted to be a part of."

Hugh put his hand on Slim's shoulder. He'd clearly never heard *this story* before.

"I didn't know anything about the military, but Dykes convinced me. And I wanted to trust him. I had to get out. So the next week he came over to sign the papers. And just like that I was part of Stoke Ridge Military. Momma was so high she took off her shirt on account of the heat. She didn't know what she was signing but she did it just the same. I packed my sports bag, and just like that I was gone."

Slim sipped his whiskey.

"He was nice in the beginning. I felt like there was a connection. It was the first time someone ever cared about me, you know? Uncle Chandler, I called him. Uncle Sarge. But that lasted about three weeks. Then he started making me come to his office—in the daytime to do push-ups, at night to sleep—as long as I stuck close, he said he'd protect me. So there I was, the new kid, a scrawny thirteen-year-old, almost happy 'cause I thought I was safe."

Slim shook his head. "Bastards. It was a military academy after all. They shave your head and tell you to obey. You eat the same thing every day, wake up at the same hour. I was used to being outside, having my freedom to walk around, and it started to weigh on me. The more Dykes told me the kids didn't like me, the more I relied on him, the more I felt alone. Dykes wanted me all to himself. He was damn lonely, too. He put me on the JV basketball team because he was the coach. But Dykes is jealous, you know, so once he saw me building camaraderie with the team? That's when he got obsessed with keeping me around after practice. You could see it in his eyes. He'd put me in a head lock and give me noogies. I didn't really question why he didn't do it to the others."

Hugh's hand was still on Slim's shoulder.

"When we lost games, he made us do push-ups in his office."

"The whole team in his office?" Hugh asked.

"Yeah, it was small. But that just gave him an excuse to tell us to take our shirts off. It was hot and there wasn't a fan. So he'd sit behind his desk that had a stuffed opossum on it, screaming at us until we were exhausted."

"Stuffed opossum?" Hugh asked.

"Pink gums and glaring teeth. It was creepy for sure. Seemed like it was staring at us. But Dykes didn't realize misery loves company, and all those late-night workout sessions bonded us cadets. We started to act out and I sort of became the ring leader."

Slim sipped his drink until the glass was empty. "You can't train kids to kill without giving 'em a reason. Do you have a bathroom, Lockart? I need to take a piss."

The Beast and I exchanged a look.

"Shit, Lockart," he said. "You're really getting him to spill his guts."

"The whiskey helps. So do you, I'm sure."

I poured three glasses of water. We sat in silence listening to the rain.

Slim returned from the bathroom. "That's his cabin out back? All run down?"

"Sure is," I answered. "In those brambles and bushes. I've only been there once. Don't fancy going back again."

"Where was I?" Slim chugged the water.

"You wanted to get back at Dykes?"

"Right. Funny how the smallest men can make you feel like *you're* the small one. Dykes picked on me in particular, but always behind closed doors. I don't need to go into details, but he treated me like an abusive boyfriend who buys his girl jewelry to make up for her black eye. He took me out to dinner at Bojangles and Golden Corral. He bought me shoes at Foot Locker and clothes at JCPenney. For a time it worked 'cause the other kids got jealous. And since they knew Dykes would defend me, they started to fear me. But I didn't like being feared—you end up alone, just like Dykes. And that's of course what Dykes wanted—to be the most feared man at Stoke Ridge."

Slim scratched at his faded neck scar. "I realized the other kids didn't fear me so much as they felt sorry for me. But once I hit puberty, it was a whole different ball game. I grew eleven inches junior year—five feet seven to six feet five. Dykes' mistake was sticking with our class of cadets instead of taking on a new group of young'uns. He didn't intimidate us in the same way anymore. He no longer had the same power. And you know what happens when pathetic men lose their power . . . they double down. He started abusing me psychologically. Somehow it made me even more attached. I know it isn't right, but it's the truth. I couldn't let go. Stockholm syndrome or some shit. And then after nine-eleven, Bush Junior started talking about war. I knew I'd be on the first transport out 'cause I was the best cadet in the academy. So you better believe, when Dykes realized I was leaving? He lost his shit."

We didn't ask any questions. We waited for Slim to gather his thoughts.

"Fighting a war on the other side of the world started to seem like a mighty fine alternative," Slim resumed. "But I was only seventeen. I still had to survive another year."

"Did anyone at Stoke Ridge know this was happening?"

"General Haith, the director, was a kind man. He promised that he'd talk to some of the higher-ups and see if he couldn't get me fighting in Iraq before my birthday. Those last months at Stoke Ridge were brutal. I fought in Fallujah, sure, but that time was the scariest in my life. . . anyway, by the time I graduated, I was the best goddamn soldier Stoke Ridge had ever known. I channeled all that bullshit into becoming a warrior. I'm not proud of it, but like I said, you can't train kids to kill without giving 'em a reason. By the time they shipped me out to Fallujah? I was ready to kill."

Slim's demeanor shifted. "Talk about a crazy idea, right? Letting teenagers go straight from a military academy to war. No amount of training can prepare you for that shit. And you gotta remember: we'd never seen so much as a goddamn gunshot wound, let alone a street scattered with bodies and limbs. People's heads exploding, brains oozing out, seeing your buddies filled with holes like Swiss cheese . . . can I have another whiskey, Lockart? Desensitize would be the closest word for it. Technology these days . . . you put a guy up in a helicopter and throw him some night-vision goggles and he'll shoot the grainy silhouettes on the ground, no problem. You ever wonder why I refuse to play all those shooter games, Hugh? You don't want to know just how realistic they are."

All of us were mildly drunk.

"See, *terrorist* is just a word they use to convince you to pull the trigger. I mean, how else are they supposed to get teenagers to shoot at twelve-year-old boys? It was a shitty situation, I know, but I did what I was told, and thanks to George, Dick and Donald's wisdom, I ended up with a bullet through the jugular and a ticket home."

"Jesus," Hugh said. "But you went back for a second tour?"

"You better believe it. I heard the term once: auto-telic experience. And there's nothing like facing death to make you feel alive. During my first rehabilitation, General Haith visited my bedside. I think he felt guilty. He knew I had nobody. Before shipping out for my second tour, Haith came with me to say goodbye to my mother."

"What a way to go," Slim shook his head. "Turns out she'd discovered edibles. Ingested a whole batch of brownies before going out in the heat to do what she loved most. We found her dead in the grass. She never did buy a blade protector for that damn lawn mower. Her foot looked like diced onions when we found her. She probably was too stoned to even feel it, laying there, watching the grass turn red. Come to think of it, that was the last time I saw Haith. I should get back in touch. He told me, you aren't in control of what life throws at you, only in how you respond. That stuck with me through my second tour and my years at UNC. And now here I am, Dykes is back, and what am I supposed to do, Lockart?"

9

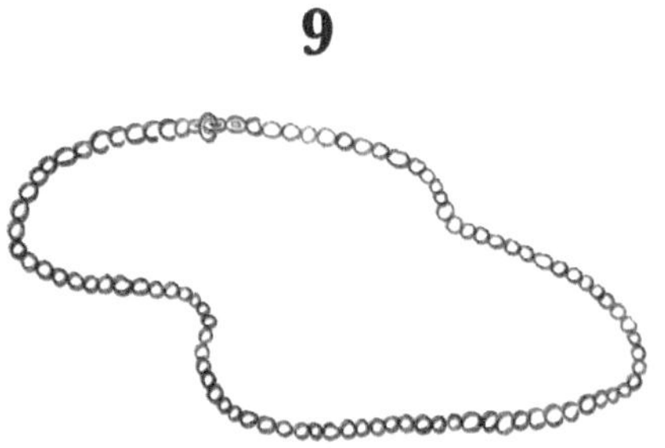

The Painted Lake

A waft of must followed him in: mothballs and booze, the consummate alcoholic. Despite his six-foot-frame, Dykes had all the markings of a small, pathetic man. He hunched his shoulders when he walked and he swung his arms like a gorilla. He finished sentences with question marks, his voice nasal, grating, and tenuous. Come rain or shine, the mosquitoes or the heat, you could be sure Dykes looked for a reason to complain. He had no chutzpah, no balls, no tact, and no charm. He woke up every day believing he was the victim, and though he'd inherited a fortune and a mansion to boot, just like his parents, he never realized a bigger house means an emptier one, too. Without any ambition, purpose, or self-respect, Dykes lubricated his sorrow at my bar.

"Could there be more to Dykes than meets the eye?" The Beast asked.

"No, there's less," Slim said.

"You don't know about his parents though, do you? And that means you don't know the half of it—you ever heard of the Painted Lake?"

"Can't say that I have. He never talked about his youth. He only ever mentioned Mr. Charles . . ."

"Ah, Mr. Charles," I said. "His chauffeur until thirteen. Apparently he liked to play marbles and watch Dykes dance . . ."

"You mentioned something about a lake?" The Beast asked.

"It used to be called Dykes Pond," I answered. "Renamed the Painted Lake on account of the LGBT community. It's quite the story. One second, I'll put some music on. Always nice to have a good soundtrack to a story, isn't it?"

For a moment no one spoke except for Robert Johnson

You better come on, in my kitchen,
well it's goin' to be rainin' outdoors.

"Sasha Dykes was a self-described *après-gardiste*. The term didn't exist outside of her mind. Less than one hundred people ever saw her art, but part of the allure was thinking her art was valuable 'cause it was rare. She'd been born Sasha Jenkins and had lived above the sewers of New York, just early enough to witness the twilight of the Dadaist movement. By eighteen she was calling herself a concept artist, taking pride in imaginary paintings and drawings that could hypothetically be drawn. Unaware that she had to believe in what she was doing, and while most Dadaist artists were moving on to surrealism, Sasha continued to take pride in her concepts. Sasha was a buffoon, plain and simple, but she was also beautiful, which kept her on the fringes of the popular artist crowd. She wanted to seem nonchalant while doing everything to be seen, and so at twenty-three—when she met a rich man who liked expensive art by the name of Trent Dykes—she quickly fell in love with the lifestyle of attending trendy galas, where she could peddle her artsy concepts to moneyed socialites, but it didn't last long. Trent's work, pharmaceuticals, soon relocated them to North Carolina, where he promised his newlywed she could make all the art she wanted in their mansion next to a man-made pond."

"What started as an empty relationship turned into an empty marriage. Trent wooed his bodacious lover with jewelry and fine wines. They slept back to back and argued more than they hugged. Trent worked late nights in Raleigh, where, as Chandler always brings up, he cheated on Sasha all the time. Chandler walked in on his father receiving a blow job more than once—from a maid in the laundry room, from a catering staffer behind the woodshed—twice—and Sasha Dykes herself in Trent's air-conditioned office in Raleigh. He walked in on his mother on her knees under the desk, her ass sticking out. She was wearing a skirt. His father told him to watch. The car ride home was quiet. His mother had a new necklace on."

"Once Trent grew tired of Sasha's mouth, and built her a toy for her concept art: a large tower hanging over The Painted Lake. The thirty-foot wooden structure built like a medieval siege unit had a rickety wooden ladder leading to a diving platform up top. It loomed over floating plastic cordons containing different colored paints—reds, blues, greens, and yellows like chocolate pudding skins atop the water. A camera on a tripod stood on the other side of the pond, set to time-capture the fateful day when Sasha would finally jump. She worked exclusively in a red and blue polka-dotted dress and spent most of her days in contemplation, full of anti-depressants, dangling her feet off the edge of the tower. For years she just sat there, day in and day out, and then one day she decided to jump. Little Chandler witnessed it from his bedroom. Trent wasn't around. The splash was colorful, if underwhelming. Sasha quickly got out of the water and sprinted up the hill with her camera and put the singular photo into a scrapbook entitled ART. Sasha spent all of her time by the pond, envisioning her second jump, ignoring of the needs of little Chandler. Dykes learned about loneliness but not the art of solitude. He liked spending time in the bathtub because of the warmth and the silence. Somehow he liked the idea that his parents wouldn't know if he'd drowned. By seven years old he was making his own lunches. At school, he never had anything good enough to trade for cookies."

"And then one day, as if his parents' neglect wasn't enough, they hired a chauffeur named Mr. Charles. Mr. Charles picked Chandler up from school at three o'clock on the dot. At first, he made him after-school snacks, played marbles, and ran him baths. Sometime just before puberty things got bad. Dykes has never said what exactly happened, but one night, Chandler got into the liquor cabinet, and almost drowned in the bath.

"So he tried to kill himself?" The Beast asked.

"That's not how he saw it," I replied. "He never told me if he'd done it on purpose, just that he 'wanted to fall asleep, turn it off.' His dad ended up pulling him out of the bathtub after coming home late. Chandler used the opportunity to twist the story. Said Mr. Charles was with Sasha down by the pond. Trent fired Mr. Charles and enrolled Chandler at Stoke Ridge Military Academy."

Robert Johnson crooned:

> *Wonder could I bear apologize?*
> *Or would she sympathize with me?*
> *Wonder could I bear apologize?*

I looked at Slim in the waning summer light, trying to guess what he was thinking.

"We won't even make it to Greensboro before it hits," The Beast was at the window.

The sky looked mean. Black clouds rolled in and grumbled about. The rain had started up but the lightning remained hidden. Still, thunder began to rumble along the rooftop.

"You think it's gonna be worse than Fran?" Slim asked. "I haven't seen a real storm in years . . ."

"Neither have I," The Beast said. "I say we wait it out."

"You boys are welcome to stay here," I offered. "There's a bedroom upstairs. Jane will be coming around to give us the update, anyhow."

Robert Johnson plucked his strings for a time.

"So what happened to Trent and Sasha?" The Beast sipped a fresh whiskey.

"After years of contemplating a second splash, Sasha Dykes decided to make her art public. Chandler was fourteen, home for vacation from Stoke Ridge. It may have been Trent who coerced her to finally jump. See, party-goers were no longer impressed with Sasha's concept art, and Trent had his own reasons for collecting the event funds. He promised her more jewelry and Botox, and planned the party weeks before even asking for her thoughts. North Carolina's rich and entitled poured tens of thousands into the *The Painted Lake: The Gravity is Art Gala*."

"The main event was to be centered on a seventy-six-foot jump into the multicolored pond to guarantee the most vibrant of splashes. As Sasha climbed the ladder to reach the summit, looking down at the newly bought rubber containment booms filled with reds, greens, blues, and yellows, she waved at the double-chinned Kens and wrinkled Barbies squinting up towards the Carolina blue, sipping beers and mimosas, respectively. At the top of the structure, Sasha removed her faded polka-dot dress with drama, and watched it float down."

"One can only hope she found purpose high above her painted lake. 'I'm off to glory!' She shrieked, and jumped."

"Jesus," Slim said.

"The splash was majestic—a colorful eruption—but being an unrealized concept artist, it never occurred to Sasha that if you make the jump higher, you gotta make the pond deeper, too. It took thirty-three seconds for Trent to jump in. Most guests thought it was all part of the spectacle. By the time two members of the wait staff managed to drag Sasha's lifeless body out of the painted waters, most guests were already making the tragedy about them. Chandler watched dozens of drunken party guests speak to local news crews, recounting what had happened as if the tragedy was their own. Soon enough, they all returned to their mansions in Asheville and Southern Pines and their penthouses in Manhattan, where they sat in lofted apartments filled with floor pillows and mineral water bottles and waxed poetic about how amazing it was to see someone *literally die for her art* and how *that* was *true art* and how the *'culture bearers'* *of today could learn a thing or two from the late Sasha Dykes*, the Dadaist who was, in the words of a famed buxom art critic, 'a hero amongst us all.'"

The Beast shook his head. "What a shame. I'm guessing Trent didn't suddenly become father of the year, either?"

"Far from it," I answered. "He was remarried within the year to the buxom art critic. He sold the house, paid Stoke Ridge to look after Chandler full-time, and got a job in Manhattan in pharmaceutical finance. He died a few years later on September eleventh."

"Holy hell," The Beast replied. "Well, that explains a lot."

"Yeah, but it doesn't excuse anything," Slim said.

"No, it doesn't," The Beast replied. "But understanding isn't forgiving, is it? And perspective matters—you know that more than most, Slim. Losing both parents like that? I wouldn't wish it on my worst enemy."

10

Chez Nous

Jennifer Dawton and Winston Fields used to run a quaint diner off Old Highway 86. It was a long, winding road slicing through dense forests and verdant meadows and golden pastures covered in rolls of hay. The barns used to hold pigs and sheep, but by the time Hugh Dawton-Fields (AKA The Beast) was born, there were mostly machines. Still, when the Dawton-Fields relocated back in the eighties, there were no sub-divisions or shopping centers or cookie-cutter homes, just tick-infested forests filled with agile and frightened deer, and everywhere the cicadas chirping and the bees buzzing amid the quiet rustle of trees, and pollen irritating the eyes and thunderstorms flooding shallow waters. The region used to be filled with people who knew the lay of the land. They didn't wear earplugs while mowing the lawn, or goggles to use a tractor, or gloves to weed, or bug spray in the yard. The Dawton-Fields bought local, but not 'cause they were virtue signaling: "going green" was as obvious as dishwashing by hand.

Their beloved family-owned restaurant was called Chez

Nous. It stood alone in a clearing, down a dusty road lined with grass. It was a small two-story home with a screened in porch. The first floor had been renovated to give the feel of a classic diner, but the tables were small and round like in French cafés.

"The goal was a memorable experience," Hugh recalled while we snacked on peanuts to offset the whiskey. "And part of that experience is losing track of time."

Chez Nous was a favorite among local artists and musicians, who often sat on the porch in white rocking chairs and drank sweet tea. It was a popular place on account of the family feel and the honest prices, but those who knew about cuisine also knew about this French secret down south. According to Southern Living, Chez Nous was among the best in French fusion on account of its "haute-cuisine creations with a down-home feel." The Dawton-Fields won multiple awards for the place, including Southern Living's Meal of the Year Award for their honey-glazed duck breast in a red wine reduction alongside green bean casserole, a goat cheese soufflé, cornbread brioche, and the chef's choice of wine.

Jennifer Dawton had started out as a bio major before falling in love with cooking. After graduating from Duke University in the mid-sixties, she moved with her fiancé, Winston, to Paris. And there, under the trees of Canal Saint Martin, they drank Côtes du Rhône and frequented the famous Marché d'Aligre, where they learned how to properly sear a duck, grill shrimp, and roast a chicken, how to pick the right sauces for a steak tartare, and how to judge a baguette by bringing it right up to the ear and giving it a slight squeeze in the middle to verify the crunch. They became *amateurs* in the best French sense of the word—lovers—before moving back to North Carolina to start a family.

When Hugh Dawton-Fields was born, he didn't scream. The nurse said he had some kind of mischief in his eyes, and as a boy he snuck away to be alone after dinner.

"They moved to downtown Carrboro in the beginning," Hugh recalled. "Lived with a couple of hippies. But they didn't like having to always eat vegan, not for long, so they bought a place in the countryside and started Chez Nous."

Slim listened intently. He hadn't heard this before.

Jennifer and Winston renovated the whole place. Winston literally broke his back once when he fell from a ladder. Chez Nous was finished by the time Hugh turned three, and within six months they were able to buy a second place down the street, keeping the upstairs bedroom to sleep in on busy weekend nights.

"I slept on two sleeping bags, bordered by pillows on the floor." Hugh swallowed hard.

After a stressful year full of success at Chez Nous, Hugh developed a skin condition that demanded his parents' full attention. "Once I got better they reopened the restaurant and started to work weekends again. But they never went back to full-time . . . they knew how important it was for me to have them around. I was shy when I started school and got made fun of for being so tall. The only thing I had then was the basketball court."

"How tall were you?" Slim asked.

"Five feet five by the time I was ten."

"Was that where you got the nickname?"

"The Beast? No. They called me Mr. Munster."

"From the show on Nick at Nite?" Slim wondered.

"Yeah. 'Cause of my deep voice, too. I didn't really hang around other kids until I was fifteen. I didn't mind it though . . . mostly remember helping out in the kitchen and playing basketball out back. I liked being alone."

"You spent all day playing?"

"All day basketball. All evening cooking. I was happy in the kitchen. Didn't much like going to school. I think my parents worried. No one wants to see their kid getting called names. But what were they gonna do? They couldn't sit there with me in class and defend me. They just made sure to ask how my day was when I got home. Not just what I did, but how I actually felt. They were more like friends, really. They instilled the lessons early on."

If they'd had a bad day, they'd honor it instead of suppress it—instead of taking out their frustration on Hugh when he spilled the milk, they'd sit the four-year-old down and explain how if-we-seem-upset-honey-well-it's-not-your-fault-it's-just-been-a-tough-day-at-the-restaurant-'cause-the-steamer's-broken. And even though the four-year-old could barely understand what they were saying, he could *feel* that their frustration wasn't about him; and if there were a problem between Jennifer and Winston—say, a screaming match over when it was best to clean the kitchen—they'd apologize for the cursing and the yelling and bashfully conclude that in the end the best strategy is to clean while you cook.

The Dawton-Fields brought out the best in each other.

Since they treated their child with respect and responsibility, they never made him pick sides because it was never about who could win. Cooking was the primary teaching tool for their child, but not the last. The rule in the kitchen was simple enough: if someone was cooking, *everyone* was cooking, so from six-years-old onward, Hugh made the salad dressing while Jennifer cut the vegetables and Winston layered the lasagna. Each time they sat down for dinner, they held each other's hands in a circle, sharing a moment of silence before digging in.

"They taught me to stay present and focused on the task. To take care with everything, from preparation to presentation to cleaning up *before* the meal was ready. Multitasking was fine as long as I made sure never to leave the handle of the frying pan sticking out from the stove top."

"Sounds like a damn nice childhood," Slim said dreamily.

"Yeah, of course. I don't deny it. But a kid isn't just the product of his parents, right? You forget: I went to public schools, overcrowded and underfunded, governed by disillusioned and underpaid teachers. Like you, Slim, I was lost when I got to high school. My whole body was changing and I had no idea what was going on. Suddenly, I was huge. How do you tell a kid to be comfortable when he's nearly seven feet tall? I grew nine inches in less than two years. That's when I started getting a lot of attention for basketball. The varsity coach wanted me on the team. He'd never seen me play but he figured my height could be useful. And it made me feel good to be useful."

"And your teammates?" Slim asked. "Were you close?"

"Not really, no. They'd known each other since they were six. Always hung out after games, but never invited me. Plus they were way too serious about it, basketball that is . . . they were into AAU and all the Nike camps and stuff, and I didn't have the team spirit coach always talked about . . . still played like I was in the backyard—just for fun. But I was seven feet. I didn't have to try too hard to be the best in the state. I'd watched Jordan documentaries since I was a kid, like everyone of my generation. In the beginning I was too aggressive, partly 'cause I wanted to get back at the same kids that called me Mr. Munster. But I got over that pretty quickly, mostly because they were on my team and eventually I got good. That's when they started calling me The Beast."

"So the team gave you your nickname?"

"Yeah. Somewhere along the way. I broke a teammate's nose, kind of by accident. Or maybe it was his wrist."

"By accident?" Slim asked.

"Yeah, well . . . I wanted to hurt him, but not that badly."

"What'd he do?"

"He made fun of me and my dad's love for French cooking. But by senior year, it was all good. The college scouts started calling my parents day and night. It was crazy the amount of attention I got once people started thinking about money. They were saying I was the best center to come out of high school since Shaq. My parents didn't think it was in my best interest to skip college, didn't trust anyone who was willing to bribe a teenager out of an education. And they got sick of it really quickly, what with the phone ringing day and night. They never let me do magazine covers or any of that. They said I was too young to have a public image. And I was fine with that. I preferred being quiet. It's exhausting to have people staring at you all the time—and when you're seven foot they already do. Scouts were always coming to eat at Chez Nous. There was this one recruiter from the University of Tennessee who was incessant. He spent a whole summer at the restaurant. Fakest smile I've ever seen. My mom finally put a laxative in his shrimp and grits."

"So how'd you end up at UNC?" I asked, refilling the peanuts and water glasses.

"It was the only school that didn't pressure me. Duke was nice too, but they already had a stacked front court. Plus, UNC was closer to my parents and they said I'd play immediately."

"I remember seeing those 'Dawn of The Beast' T-shirts freshman year," Slim recalled.

"Yeah, that's when the nickname really caught on— T-shirts and posters and all the rest of it. The whole thing was surreal. Dick Vitale screaming, "IT'S THE BEAST, BABY!" But you know that feeling when you're at a really good party but all you want to do is leave? My parents knew me better than anyone else in the world, and sensed I didn't feel it. Not that I didn't like it, just that my life didn't revolve around the result of the game. One of the last things my dad ever told me to remember was a quote by Dr. J: 'Being a professional is doing the things you love to do on the days you don't feel like doing them.'"

Slim couldn't help but amend the phrase. "Yeah, that

and a couple growth spurts, a forty-inch vertical, and a massive wing span. Not to mention staying healthy . . ."

"I still think about that sentence every day." The Beast's eyes welled up.

Despite the jovial music in the background—I'd switched to Django Reinhardt's "Minor Swing"—the energy had shifted. I made a point to turn the music down so it wouldn't overpower Hugh's next words.

"The night they died we got in a fight. It was in late February, 2009, just before March Madness of my junior year, but I was at the restaurant helping them work late. They were teaching me how to perfect a new soufflé recipe for a big gala at the American Embassy in Paris . . . I don't know what started the fire. Maybe a gas leak? I just wish we hadn't fought that night. It was so stupid . . . I was frustrated—the soufflé kept deflating. My dad told me that's what happens when you've got your feet in two different worlds. I wanted to prove him wrong—that I could cook just as well as I could play. UNC was the favorite for March Madness, but I really wanted to go to France to represent Chez Nous in April. And that's when my dad quoted Dr. J—he said I couldn't just walk in here and expect it to be easy. He said cooking takes patience and experience and time. My poor mom was just trying to help out . . . she said not to think of it as a competition—that I had to cook with love. I knew it was true, but it sounded so patronizing. She was always so optimistic. So I yelled at her. That's when my dad told me to get out of the kitchen, and so I shoved him. He fell back into a shelf and knocked over a couple of pots. I can still see my mom's eyes—that's what kills me. Even then, at that moment, she managed to be calm. 'Get some sleep, Hugh,' she said. She put her hand on my shoulder and followed my dad up to the bedroom above the restaurant."

The Beast's voice was shaky. His eyes remained glued to the bar. "I went for a drive to cool off. The firetrucks were at the house when I got back. I was devastated. I ate cold meatloaf for weeks, and stopped showing up for practice. Coach Brees came a few times to leave groceries, kept insisting we talk about it, trying to force me to play, saying it would help me move on. But he was angry. I knew all he cared about was winning the championship. But I just didn't want to play anymore. That's when I decided to put both my feet into cooking. Working at The Skillet was a new beginning. That summer I went through all of the family recipes. It was the only way I could feel close to them again. "

Hugh Dawton-Fields grieved in his own way. He seared duck and grilled summer vegetables; he sautéed prawns and stuffed tomatoes; he fried gnocchi with onions and zucchinis marinated in Moroccan spices and crème fraîche; he made tortellini stuffed with lobster and sun-dried tomatoes; he drizzled the finest olive oil, balsamic vinegar, and mustard concoction on top of summer salads made with honey seared apples and fennel. He took care not only to make the food, but also to present it as his own, often applying his father's technique of flipping a small white bowl filled with rice upside down, placing golden-brown onions ever-so-gently on top of a homemade burger topped with a dash of sea salt and perhaps a sprig of rosemary for decoration, or hanging a single bay leaf on an oven-baked chicken breast, not 'cause he ate it, but 'cause the aesthetic was also important, ". . . and only then, once it's decorated, can you slice through the meat with the edge of your fork."

"I became an amateur chef in the Latin sense of the word. I loved every minute of it. When I was cooking, they felt alive. I listened to Chet Baker and Miles Davis and took my time eating, as if every bite or sip brought them back. I remembered jumping in their bed, and playing gymnastics in the morning. My father used to lift me up to the basketball hoop. At night, my mom would gently press on my eyelids just before I fell asleep. In the mornings, they brewed milky cups of Earl Grey tea. I still do it to this day, just like my father used to make, taking care to put the sugar and the tea bag in first, then pouring in the water and only later adding the milk."

"It's true," Slim said. "I've seen you do it just like that."

The Beast looked at Slim and smiled. "I haven't talked about that to anyone. Coach Brees never did let me grieve after the fire. He won't let me move on to this very day."

"Soon he'll be out of your life for good," Slim responded.

"Yeah …" The Beast didn't seem so sure. "Not soon enough. Between Dykes and Coach Brees, we've got quite the past to leave behind."

"You know," I interjected. It was time I revealed an inconvenient truth about their predicament. "I didn't want to tell you earlier because, well, it wasn't the right time, but after hearing all this . . . yesterday I decided to go down to Dykes' cabin for a welfare check. He hadn't come around in a few days, which is a red flag for a drunkard. While I was down there, I saw something you both should know about."

11

Meet The Prospects

When I got to Dykes' cabin, I peered through the open front door that led into the dreary living room. I could see crumpled papers, scattered peanuts, empty pizza boxes, and bottles of Red Label Johnny Walker on the floor. There was an old Toshiba TV illuminating the room with its fuzzy screen, shedding gray light on newspaper clippings covering the carpet. I could make out various stories of Slim's military discharge, the war in Iraq, restaurant reviews of Chez Nous, local articles about Hugh's career at UNC, the Coach Brees scandal, and one piece entitled 'What Went Wrong?' There were also two cut-out headlines taped to the wall that stood out: 'Coach Jim Brees Pleads Silence in Assault Case,' and 'Stoke Ridge Military Academy to Hold Memorial for General Don B. Haith.'

"Haith?" Slim asked.

"I'm afraid so. It seems he died in a fire last fall. The authorities said it was arson. Anyhow, Dykes' cabin is creepy, I'll tell you that much. There was little else in the living room save a yellow pillow and dirty laundry. In the bedroom, a mattress and a single red lamp on the floor, and lots of photos of you two boys on the wall, threaded together with red string like you see in those detective movies. The pictures of you, Slim, were mostly Polaroids. Most of them had your face circled in red marker. The same goes for you, Hugh, except that the photos of you were mostly low-quality Internet printouts. There was one document in the center of the wall that stood out the most, though. It was the centerpiece of his whole conspiracy theory, whatever it is, a list filled with bold, black names:

B.A.M. LIST
~~Mom and Dad~~
Slim
~~General Haith~~
~~Saddam~~
The Facebook Team
The Beast

"What a fucking creep," Slim said. "He had that same list in his office at Stoke Ridge."

"And you said General Haith's name was crossed off?" The Beast asked.

"Him and Saddam's," I replied. "And his parents, too, of course. But as I was studying it, I heard this loud, hissing sound, like a snake or something . . . I noticed some type of cage with a couple of pizza boxes on top of it. There was something inside, hissing and skulking—"

"Was it a cat?"

"I wish. A fiendish opossum. Started slamming itself up against the cage, sticking its snout through the grating, gnawing at the metal, trying every which way to get out. Razor sharp fangs as well . . . too many little teeth inside its mouth."

"I didn't think you could domesticate an opossum," The Beast said.

"You can't," I replied. "It was acting mighty feral. Could even have rabies."

"Dykes had a stuffed opossum in his office at Stoke Ridge," Slim said. "He called him Larry."

"Larry, that's it," I replied. "He's always asking if he can bring Larry some peanuts. Seems he hasn't moved on. Anyway. A terrifying creature. But after seeing the likes of Larry the Opossum, I wasn't trying to stick around, but just as I was leaving, I noticed a flickering light from beneath the bathroom door. I heard water running, so I high-tailed it outside and peered through the bathroom window. I could only see by the flicker of a candle. Don't freak out now, all right? But there he was, naked in the steaming tub, suckling on a bottle of whiskey, silhouetted by the blue glow of his laptop screen. I figured he'd be watching porn, but then I saw it: he was watching you, Hugh."

"Me!" The Beast looked disturbed. "I've never been in porn!"

Slim looked horrified, mouth agape. "Watching Hugh? How?"

"Nothing untoward, oddly enough. It was an interview on ESPN."

"*Meet the Prospects*," The Beast said, nodding his head. "I pissed off a lot of people with that interview, nobody more than Coach Brees."

ESPN's Meet the Prospects
Hugh Dawton-Fields

"Thank you for agreeing to this, Hugh. So, before we get to the question everybody's waiting for, I have to ask: what made you agree to this interview? You've been quite adamant about your refusal to answer any—"

"I wanted to clear the air, that's all. It's time for a new chapter, you know? Time to move on from it all."

"Move on? What do you mean, if you don't mind me asking?"

"I do mind. Next question. If I hadn't agreed to doing this live, your editors would already be spinning my words for ratings."

"Fair enough. You're ready to turn the page. I understand. But last year you spoke of the possibility of not returning for senior year, of maybe never playing again. Can you speak to those who doubt you still have passion for the game?"

"Well, for starters, I came back, didn't I? I just needed a break from basketball, that's all. Like Michael Jordan said, when you lose passion for something, it's time to take a break. It was tough, you know, what with my parents passing and then the fiasco with Coach Brees."

"Would you mind telling us a bit more about that?"

"Yeah, actually, I would."

"Okay, that's fair. So what made you decide to put on the Tarheel jersey again?"

"I wanted the degree. As you'll recall, I'm a scholarship player, and what with the Coach Brees incident, well, I don't need to go into details, but I wasn't going to be able to graduate if I didn't play. But that's only part of the reason. I'm not an idiot, you know. Basketball is a dangerous sport. Injuries happen and priorities change, and I wasn't going to forego a degree simply out of principle. Losing out on money is one thing. Far more dangerous to lose your mind."

"I just have to ask, Hugh, because you said, 'forego a degree out of principle.' Which principle would that be?"

"Never mind. Next question."

"Okay. But you do bring up an interesting point. A lot of scouts have questions about your motivation for the game. How much do you love basketball?"

"Seriously? Is that a real question? I love basketball *this* much. You're trying to box me in. You want me to say I want to be a perennial all-star like Shaq or Tim Duncan. You want me to reassure the doubters that I won't end up like Olowakandi, Bargnani, or Oden. Poor guys. Expectations are a killer. But that's all the system cares about in the end, isn't it? Projections and net worth. They want to point fingers one way or the other when we players rise, fall, and then say, 'I knew it.' But life can't be predicted. We all know it's true, and still we pretend like success is all about the money."

"But surely you understand, Hugh, the NBA scouts are just talking business when they say that you—"

"No, actually, we're talking about my life."

"Yes. Okay. But you've worked so hard to get where you are. Don't you—"

"I also worked hard to graduate with honors. That doesn't mean I'm going to get a PhD. Or maybe it does. Who knows. The point is, I didn't work hard to be seven feet tall, which is the only reason most scouts are interested in me in the first place."

"Yes. That and a historic college career and the best hook shot since Kareem."

"Sure. But you know, as kids, we're told we can be anything we want to be when we grow up, and then all of a sudden, something changes. When is that moment? Thirteen? Sixteen? What about when we're thirty? Learning to choose who, and how, and where we want to be is as much a question of freedom as responsibility. I love those mornings when I wake up without anything to do. It's so, so rare. But that's the question: how do I choose to spend a day when I get to be by myself? That's what life is about, isn't it? The freedom of choosing what's right for me. And sometimes that means knowing I won't always know what the next chapter will be."

"So what are you saying?"

"I'm saying life isn't a monolith, it's a mosaic, and I'm not inter-ested in being all-consumed by *anything*, let alone basketball. Which doesn't, by the way, mean I don't love playing. But whether I get drafted by Milwaukee or Indiana or get signed by a team in France—"

"France? What are you saying? Have you been speaking to the Orlando Magic?"

"No. All I'm saying is, I'm not even through a quarter of my life yet. I'm a twenty-two-year-old who still isn't sure what he wants to be when he grows up, and that's okay. Being honest with uncertainty isn't a conclusion—it's a beginning. It gives me a chance to start asking different questions."

"But Hugh, let's be real here: you can understand how these words might worry NBA scouts. Some people might think this means you don't even *want* to play, and if that's what you're say-ing, why should anyone even draft you?"

"Maybe they shouldn't. Drafting is always a risk. But I reject the question. It's in bad faith. I could be the most passionate player in the draft, and my knee could give out in summer league. And what if I tear my Achilles? Or develop blood clots? The thing is, nobody knows, but everyone wants to pretend that twenty-some-thing-year-old players *should* know. All they want is a headline that reads *The Beast wants to win seven NBA championships and be the GOAT.* But they should be cautious about using me as a means to their end. You can't find your own life purpose in trying to mold other people. That's why I'm choosing to work with my dear friend Slim and not some hotshot agent."

"Yes, which brings me to my next question: what about the risk of mixing business with friendship? Did your friend promise you something that you weren't getting from any of the other estab-lished agents?"

"Promise me something? You don't get it, do you? That's exactly why I respect Slim's opinion: he didn't tell me anything. He just listened. When you're making these life decisions, you've got so many people telling you how to live your own life . . . you've got to surround yourself with folks who only want to see you possess yourself as you are. You know, my parents never sold the restau-rant. They got huge offers to become a franchise, to appear on TV shows, to be featured in the national press, but they never cared about all that. The thing is, most people obsessed with power believe that success is only ever about the biggest paycheck. But money is just power, and those who devote their life to power are pathetic. At best, it's a poverty of ambition, a misunderstanding of what it means to be fulfilled. And now I can see some of your producers getting red in the face, wondering why they agreed to record this live in the first place."

"Let's change subjects, shall we? What about the Charlotte Bobcats? If you fall to the fifth pick, you'll have a chance to play for Michael Jordan, and while there remain a lot of uncertain-ties about you, Hugh, everyone knows you're a big fan of number twenty-three."

"You're going to get me in trouble. Next question."

"Ha. It was worth a shot. Okay. So let's talk about your op-ed piece about student athletes in the NCAA. You were quite outspoken."

"What's there to talk about? I still am. Your viewers can go and read the piece. It's free. And it's no big mystery that the NCAA is a big business, plain and simple—and success in big business almost always comes with exploitation. You know, us athletes aren't as dumb as you may think. In 2009, the NCAA generated nearly a billion dollars using the likenesses of faces like mine without paying us a dime. I say it's high time they started treating us a bit less like property."

"Well, you do get scholarships . . ."

"In-state tuition and free shoes and lunch at the cafeteria—are you kidding? Do you know how much the UNC athletic director got paid last year? I can see your producers getting squirrelly back there, but I also know this makes for good live TV, so hear me clearly: being an NCAA athlete in 2010 is indentured servitude. Look up the definition before you scoff. Most of us come from tough backgrounds—they recruit us just like they recruit kids in the army. It's legalized thievery, and all I said in that piece is that there's no reason good business and fair business have to be mutually exclusive."

"Would you like to speak to the rumors regarding a certain someone—or some financial reason—that you decided to come back?"

"I'm not falling for that. You want me to give your viewers somebody to blame, and I'm not doing that. You should ask questions of the system, not the person. And now, I think this interview is over."

"Okay, sorry, just one final question: what about your legacy at UNC? How would you like to be remembered?"

"You know, my dad always said we're like delicate sculptures—life can fracture us—but when the bad thing happens, we still have a choice: do the cracks let the light in? Or does the darkness seep out?"

"And then, late yesterday afternoon, Dykes came in reeking of sweat and whiskey, his face swollen drunk, his hairline glistening. The man was sweating profusely—his coiffe clinging to his skull like strands of black hair in a porcelain sink. He kept harping about how he'd 'known it all along' and how he'd finally talked to Coach Brees and found out your 'true character.' I recorded him, actually. The fact is, he scared me."

"What did he say?"

"I'd rather just play you the recording while I go out back and check on his cabin again," I replied. "And once that's done, we can forget Dykes and Coach Brees for good and can get down to fixing some dinner."

I pulled out my phone, placed it on the bar, and hit play.

. .

... and I've twisted my ankle again and my knee's starting to give out—there's nothing you can do about a bum knee, by the way. Do you know how much it hurts when I'm alone in bed? My dad died on September 11th, but you don't hear me complaining about it, do you? That's because I'm a man. I'm not one of those people to cry over broken marbles. I'm not one of these ungrateful millennials who don't know what it means to suffer—I'm not some famous basketball player who doesn't even know what it's like to experience real pain. He's a tourist, that's all. I have to live with it daily. That's why I'm a man. You learn to shove it all down. Grit your teeth and take the punches. You stand there and watch. Sit there and watch, Chandler. That's what daddy used to say. And so you watch. Never listening, never playing, never so much as a goddamned hug. But anyway, Coach

Brees listened to me after the interview. I finally met him at Quiznos. And do you know what he said to me? He said I had to make sure The Beast gets to the draft. Said something about him trying to get out of a contract—something about skipping out on the draft. And you know what else he said about the punch? Said The Beast went berserk for no reason, said they were running sprints or something when Coach Brees said, 'What do I have to do, light a fire under your ass? Turn on the gas!' And then The Beast lost it. He put Coach Brees in a coma with a single punch. Can you imagine the force of that fist? That's a strong, strong boy ... mmhmm.

He's trying to steal my nephew away from me, and now the powers that be are trying to take away my Toby, too. But I won't allow it—even if they did ban me from Facebook. You don't have a Facebook account, do you, Lockart? Maybe I could open one for you? What do you say? I'd take care of all of it. It could be good for business, you know? You'd get a lot of likes. They don't understand what Toby and I have. He graduated, anyway. He's a man now. They misconstrued those messages because they didn't read them from the beginning. They take it all out of context—that's what everyone does, right? Of course it sounds weird unless you know the whole story. But they don't know about the beginning. Toby was a lonely kid, you know? His dad was a traveling businessman and his mother was a drunk. And then they take one single phrase out of context and bang! Slap a restraining order on me ... but I'm used to it. Threatening the youth's innocence . . . me? Come on! I'm the one preserving their innocence! I'm protecting Toby from the world at large.

There's some crazy stuff out there, Lockart. You gotta stay informed, right? Did you hear about those mutilated orphans in Canada? I mean things that'll make your skin crawl. What about that elementary school shooting out west? Sir, yes, sir! You gotta stay informed. We can never be too sure of what we should truly be afraid of. It's hard knowing what's most important to fear. Did you hear about that woman who got flattened by a billboard in Delaware? You gotta help me board up my windows, by the way. I think I'll stay in the bathroom tomorrow night. Probably safest in the bathtub? What time are you coming over, Lockart? I have a spare couch. Why don't I make a run to Harris Teeter, buy some microwaved meals and snacks, and you can bring your wife along. What's her name again? Oh, do you mind bringing some peanuts for Larry? He gets petrified during thunderstorms. Just like Toby. Anyway. We'll wait out the storm together, and then I'll head up to Milwaukee to save my nephew. The Beast exposed himself in that interview. He's a wolf in sheep's clothing. Someday soon, it'll all be over.

12

Storm's a Comin'

Hurricane Beverly was upon us. Thunder rumbled and lightning cracked. The rain came in heaps. I sprinted across the muddy ground behind the bar to salvage Jane's wind-chimes, untangling the strings from branches. The entire tree line swayed like an arboreal behemoth, heaving back and forth in the horizontal rain. I squinted through the rain to survey Dykes' cabin, camouflaged in the forest shadows, but I couldn't see any glare coming from the TV. There were wooden boards stacked up on the side of his cabin, but none of the windows were properly protected. His rusty pickup was parked out front, which usually meant Dykes was home. Maybe he was in the bathtub, soaking like a prune, or maybe he was drunk, talking to Larry the Opossum.

As soon as I came back inside the front door jingled and creaked. Cool, wet air rushed into the bar. Slim and The Beast stood up instinctively, their chests puffed out.

My wife Jane smiled and took off her dripping raincoat,

shaking off the water before hanging it on the wall.

Her long gray hair cascaded over her shoulders.

"Storm's a comin'! That must be your boys' Jeep out there? Nice to see someone other than the sergeant in the bar!" Jane craned her head when she shook hands with Slim and The Beast. "Nice to meet you, Slim. As for you, Hugh, well I know who you are. You know I used to go to Chez Nous all the time? Even met your parents a couple of times. Nice folks, a real tragedy. But knowing your parents, they're smiling down on you right now. Best food in the state in my opinion. Ever thought about re-opening it? I heard a rumor you're quite the cook yourself," she ended with a smile.

"Pleasure to meet you too, ma'am—"

"And polite, too! But there's no need for formalities out here. Call me Jane. It's less awkward—ma'am is for old ladies with Southern drawls. Excuse me for interrupting, looks like you boys were in quite the conversation. But see my husband here is fixing to be put out on account of the storm."

"Put out? How's that?" I poured her a glass of whiskey and dried myself off with a bar towel.

"You've gotta look out the window from time to time, honey," She joked. "It's raining mighty hard out there. You know I-40's already flooding. Honey, when'd you put the painting up?" Jane sipped her whiskey and walked over to *Nighthawks*.

"Just a few days ago. Got it framed and all," I told her.

"That you did," Jane said. "And it's about time! He knows it's one of my favorites . . . me and the rest of the country, right? But there's something to it, isn't there? Why it's so popular? That's what I learned in Chicago . . . some types of beauty transcend the cliché."

"Jane was an art history major . . . liable to talk your head off!"

Jane laughed. "If you can't speak freely about what you love, well then what *can* you talk about?" Jane raised her glass. "You see how the light touches all the objects?"

Slim and The Beast walked over to the wall.

"Edward Hopper," Jane said. "I used to stand in front of it for hours. Not looking, but watching—that's the difference with good art. See the light pouring out into the darkness? How they seem to be hiding from something in the night? I tried to find the place once. Inspired by a restaurant where two streets meet, Hopper said. Well, as you can imagine, I never found it—maybe it never even existed. But does it matter? It still exists on this wall. That's the beauty of art, in my opinion, anyhow. What do you boys think about it?"

"That one man has no face . . . seems like a stranger in the diner," Slim said.

"Well, you can't see his face, you're right. Who knows what he looks like."

"The man and the woman don't seem to know each other either," The Beast said. "Definitely looks like they're hiding out."

The Beast peered into the painting. "There's no entrance. There's a door to another room, but how do they get out?"

"I didn't think you'd catch that!" Jane said. "You've

got quite the eye. No exit, you're right. Unless they jump through those windows, of course. Speaking of windows, how *exactly* were you planning to board 'em up on your own, honey? Good thing these boys showed up!"

"I was just thinking it was about time to get those boards up on the windows."

"Oh you *were just thinking?*" Jane put her hands on Slim and The Beast's backs. "I swear, sometimes I wonder what the man would do without me!" Jane laughed. "You know the wind's gonna be over one hundred and fifty miles per hour? Listen, you two boys, why don't you go outside and bring in those boards from the back of my truck? I heard the screen door creak when I walked in. I thought you were gonna fix it honey . . ."

"Well I did fix it, but when they came in—"

"You know how I feel about excuses . . . they only satisfy those who make 'em. Run out back to get the nails for the plywood, boys. I'll fix that hinge for good."

Slim and The Beast gathered the wood from the back of Jane's truck as I went to look in the wood shed for a couple of hammers and nails. We made quick work of boarding up the windows in the front, and, thanks to Jane, by the time we were finished, the screen door didn't creak anymore.

"Well, I've got to get going if I don't wanna get stuck here all night with you boys," Jane said. "I've got research to do for my new sculpture. Trying to reflect light through multiple prisms à la Hopper. I'll do what I can until the power goes out. Honey, you be wise with these boys. If you need something you call me on the walkie-talkie. I'll see you boys in the morning then. You're not going anywhere far tonight in this storm."

I walked Jane through the rain to her pickup.

"You going to be alright hunkering down with those boys tonight?" She asked me through the cracked car door.

"We'll be just fine. See you in the morning." I kissed her on the forehead and ran back into the bar.

"Catharsis?" Slim was saying.

Kind of Blue by Miles Davis was playing on the speaker.

"Right. And it could be God, or many gods, whatever," Hugh replied.

"Glass of water?" I asked.

"Sure, why not. You might not be religious, but you've still gotta respect it, Slim. You don't have to agree to respect their effort … "

"But that's why you get people like Dykes," Slim disagreed with his friend. "All the extremists. What's this obsession with always having to listen to everybody, even bigots? I always hated anthropology."

"But can't you see the problem with that?" Hugh said. "You think you're better off *not* knowing what makes Sergeant Dykes tick? Excluding people's opinions never works out in the long run. Just because Dykes is 'crazy' doesn't mean you shouldn't try to understand him. The problem is he thinks he's right, but you think you're right, too—no, of course not, of course he's not right—but when it's all said and done, that's not the point, is it?"

"Yeah, yeah, okay. Recognize that it's all subjective, anthropology, blah, blah, blah. But is it? I don't know. You don't have to be right for some people to be wrong, do you? I mean, I'll listen to those people seeking truth, but not the ones with a preconceived answer before they even begin the search."

"So according to you he's seeking truth?" I asked.

"Well no … that's what I'm saying: he's not asking the right questions. He's only searching for answers to support his theory."

"And what theory is that?"

"Hell if I know," Slim replied. "But he isn't trying to find answers to better understand. And that's the problem, isn't it? The people who think they've got the answer … they can't help but reduce everything to fit their narrative."

"Well that's the point of faith right?" Hugh suggested. "To believe in something without proof? But still, come on Slim, you don't think faith is entirely worthless?"

"No, faith is necessary. That's what got me here … well, part of the way anyway. But if I've got faith, and you've got it, and Lockart's got it too, well then aren't we entitled to our own personal versions? The problem with Dykes is he's always trying to convince others 'cause he's not confident in his own opinion, and that's the difference: faith versus conviction. Convincing people that *your* version is the truth is where we get into trouble. No, the way I see it, claiming answers is desecrating something. It's the easy way out. The whole point is to question and cultivate our own gardens."

"That was Voltaire, right? Or was it Rousseau?"

"Voltaire. *Candide.* Dykes thinks he's right 'cause he's the loudest guy in the bar. That's why he was so obsessed with me, and the other cadets, and now this 'Toby' and even *you,* Hugh. He has so little faith in himself, he has to create someone else worth worshiping."

Slim paused for a moment as if he were unsure of what he'd said. "If you don't have faith in yourself, well, how are you supposed to have faith in anything, right? That's why I'm thankful for my first years at UNC . . . You know, when I first got there, I even considered going to church!"

"What's wrong with that?" Hugh asked.

"Man, there's no way a dude wearing a white robe serving you crackers and red wine has the answer. Or a dude with a long beard tying a black rope around your head and your arm. Or telling me I've got to slit a sacred goat's neck before I can eat it. I mean what are we talking about here? Really, what are we talking about? We're talking about people who actually believe they can survive their own death, putting happiness into someone else's hands, that God can justify killing, and that everything is part of some god's divine plan."

"You don't think everything happens for a reason?" Hugh interjected.

"Well hold on now, Hugh, let me finish! I was about to say, things happen for a reason 'cause you can find a reason in everything. But just 'cause you can find a reason doesn't mean it actually exists. Alive in its questions, religion dies in its answers. And that's the point of a horizon, right? It's constantly receding. I mean, you know this Hugh, I don't need to tell you twice. They're making a documentary about you based on what? On an article someone wrote three years ago? Dykes collecting shitty newspaper articles as if they held some truth about you? All this obsession with written words as if they were canon ... I don't get it. Really, I don't. Like Nietzsche said, look the other way. I mean, talk about lost in translation. Dykes doesn't have a clue about who you are, but he's convinced that he does, and why? 'Cause he wants to be sure of *something*, of anything." Thunder cracked. "And so now we've got some schizophrenic thinking he's a prophet and that he's destined to find us? Bottom line is, it's okay to believe in whatever helps us sleep at night, so long as we accept that it's also bat shit crazy."

"Is that possible, though? To believe in something you admit is irrational?"

"Of course it's possible! We do it all the time. Even atheists say a prayer when the plane's going down … I mean, if there were a god, right? Let's assume a supreme being. Do you think It gives a shit about what we're thinking? We can't know It. It's unknowable. That's why we invented faith. You know, I used to have an intellectual hard-on for Richard Dawkins, but that guy's missing the point, too. See, atheists are just as convinced that they've got the answer—they're equally delusional in the face of grandeur. And you know what really grinds my gears? They've got this smug pretentious air about 'em like they're talking down to fifth-graders, as if they've surpassed some threshold of knowledge and have seen the light. But it's still ignorance. Agnosticism, that's the truth. It's the only rational choice. I mean, Neil deGrasse Tyson is down with it . . ."

"Ah, but see what you just did? Now *you're* proselytizing!" Hugh laughed.

"No! And that's the point: agnosticism means we don't have the answer and maybe that we can't know it. And if you want to argue semantics and say that's an answer too, well then, yeah, the answer is we can't know. But maybe you've got a point in that I *am* convinced I'm right. That's part of being human, though … can't remain subjective all our life."

"I guess that's the challenge of becoming an adult, though: making a decision to go down a certain path despite your doubts . . . but maybe doubt can also force you to choose the wrong answer…"

"Are you telling me you think the NBA is the wrong path?" Slim asked.

"Did I say that? No. But sometimes I do get scared that I'll succeed in basketball and it will be nothing more than a profession."

"Well shit," Slim said. "Making a couple of million dollars a year playing a game you love sounds okay to me. I'm scared at a baseline level. I can't even consider making a decision. The more I study philosophy the more I just want a nice couch, a house, and a dog."

"Yeah, but we're young, Slim, you don't know what you—"

"We're not that young, Hugh. We're old enough to make a decision, anyway. *Old enough to repaint, young enough to sell.* We're not there yet, but you get the point. I'm sick of being transient. I want to create a life for myself. And even if that means a steady job and a partner … well why is that so bad?"

"Who said it was bad? It's just not what I want, not right now."

"Speak for yourself, Hugh. I could use a cup of tea with a nice gal. And sometimes I get scared that I'll never have it, and that I'll never find out exactly what I want 'cause I'll spend all my time ruminating about the options until it's too late to be anything but a lonely hack of a philosopher. But it's hard to move on when you don't know where you're going … You know, I think about my days playing down at the creek, our time at UNC together, even fighting in Iraq, and all those times where I felt connected that have since passed, and then it hits me that they'll never happen again. All of it's gone. And I miss the way the leaves crunched under my feet when I was a kid. And I miss the way we used to talk and eat burgers at The Skillet. And I miss the way my mom would always fall asleep on the couch and how her hand would slide off and hang down to the side. And I can see it all, of course, but that's not the same thing as living it. And then I feel like an asshole 'cause I get all nostalgic, and then I get depressed and, well shit, then I end up here, at the bar, like in that painting, hiding out."

"What do you think, Lockart?" Hugh asked.

"Well as far as I can tell," I pondered, "you're doing the right thing by asking the questions. You're considering all the possibilities, and there are a helluva lot of them. That's the beauty of being young."

"You know," Slim said. "Sometimes I spend hours lying in bed trying to find a reason to get up. I wake up and stare at the ceiling literally for hours. I start philosophizing, and then I think I'm an idiot for philosophizing instead of just getting up and making some eggs, all the while still lying in bed like a jackass."

"That's not just you, Slim. That's part of being human," Hugh replied. "You keep thinking I'm better off because I have a big decision to make, but that's equally terrifying."

"Well," Slim said, "you bringing me in as your manager

has been a game changer for me. You've got a guaranteed contract. You know, studying social theory and postulating about existence is easy 'cause I never have to decide. It's nice to have something decided for me. It's like Hemingway said, maybe I don't care what it's all about … maybe I just want to figure out a way to live in it. And if I'm really being honest? I feel most alive talking with you, Hugh. Doing exactly this. Postulating. But yeah, I'm scared of the future. I'm scared it's just a matter of time. And I'm afraid that things won't work out and I'm going to break down, just like Dykes. I mean, I've experienced some pain, but come on, not really. A couple scars here and there. Nothing profound. And so I've got all these high and mighty opinions about myself and about seeking truth, but have I been challenged to really apply them? No. I'm just a theorist, that's all. And I'm lazy 'cause I've got weed and whiskey and an Xbox. In the moment it makes me happy, but not in the long run."

There was a moment of silence—not awkward, but quiet. The rain lashed the plywood covering the windows. "All Blues" filled the bar and Cannonball Adderley's saxophone solo played to the wind.

"Slim, I have to tell you someth—"

"Just one second," Slim cut off his friend. "I'm just about finished. You know, hanging with you has been the best part of my life. If there's one thing I've learned about becoming some kind of adult it's that you have to make decisions you aren't sure will pan out."

"There's that Gide quote," Hugh recalled. "'One does not discover new lands without consenting to lose sight of the shore for a very long time.'"

"Yeah," Slim replied. "Reminds me of Eliot: 'We shall not cease from exploring and at the end of our exploration we will return to where we started and know the place for the first time.'"

"You boys are wise beyond your years," I said. "But you've got to remember to enjoy the ride."

Kind of Blue culminated with "Flamenco Sketches (Alternate Take)." We relished Miles Davis' solemn trumpet and Bill Evans' delicate piano.

13

Slim's Famous Burger

Slim showed me how to connect a phone to a new Bluetooth speaker Jane had gifted me as we gathered in the kitchen.

"And it's easy as that," he said. "Just make sure there's only one device connected at a time. Do you know this tune, Lockart?"

The lyrics started up: *Change? Shit. I guess change is good for any of us ...*

Slim's eyes lit up. "One of the best songs of all time, no doubt."

"I can't disagree with that." Hugh gave him daps and hugged him, and we listened to Tupac's "I Ain't Mad at Cha" in its entirety, bobbing our heads in silence, not exchanging a word until it was over.

"That's lyricism right there," Slim said. "Best of the modern poets."

Hugh begged to differ. "Notorious is still king in my

opinion. When it comes to lyrics, there's no contest. Can you put on 'Sky's the Limit' next?"

"Can do," Slim replied. "That's a beautiful tune, too, but if we're talking about storytelling? I prefer Tupac. When he's speaking from the heart, there's nobody like him."

"Right, exactly: *when he's being honest.*"

"Yeah, well, I'd take Tupac over any of the ego-driven bullshit that's on the radio nowadays … the whole art form is taking a turn for the worse."

"Doesn't every generation say that?" I chuckled. "Then again, I can't disagree with you. I grew up in the fifties and sixties—now *that* was a golden age for music."

"He ain't wrong," Slim said. "It's hard to argue with Otis Redding and The Beatles and Joe Cocker and Hendrix."

"Don't sleep on the nineties, though," Hugh replied. "Radiohead and Lauryn Hill and a Tribe Called Quest? Different styles, I agree, but they made the personal universal again—helped me transcend all the bullshit. What about you, Lockart? Who's at the top of your list?"

"It's hard to pick just one," I said. "My favorite pianist is Bill Evans, my favorite singer is Ella Fitzgerald, and my favorite songwriters are Lennon and McCartney … but if I had to choose one single artist to listen to until my dying day? That'd be Miles Davis."

"And I bet you have good arguments for why you think he's the best?" Slim asked.

"Well now, see, I didn't say *that*," I replied. "I just said Miles is my favorite. It's a waste of time and energy to proselytize if you ask me—makes you forget what or even why you believe what you believe in the first place. It's just a *feeling.*"

A massive BOOM set the lights flickering in the kitchen. I ran out to the front porch to see if the power lines were still intact. When I opened up the door to the front porch, I almost tumbled over an uprooted tree and its twisted limbs; one by one, I tossed them out beyond the porch into the howling wind. I corralled the screen door closed and returned to the kitchen, where I walked into a deeper level of Slim and The Beast's conversation.

"… and all of these acceptable ways to unmask what's ingrained—"

"But it was the burger that brought us together," Hugh said. "Because I could tell you weren't just there to get an autograph. No one had ever cursed at me like that before, telling me how to cook. Nobody at UNC had treated me like just another person, either—"

"Well, shit, I like my burgers the way I like 'em!" Slim laughed. "And I was definitely high that day, and I wanted a burger—I wasn't there for a goddamn autograph. And the thing is, Hugh, you didn't care who I was, either. You were willing to have an honest conversation. And honestly, I'd never met someone like you before—someone willing to be vulnerable from the beginning. I respected that."

"Yeah," Hugh gave Slim daps again. "Growing up, most of us aren't taught how to express that kind of vulnerability—I can thank my parents for that. And when it comes to the basketball court or the army? Good luck. We're just given shitty chauvinist slogans like *be a man* and *brothers in arms.*"

"And 'bros before hoes' and 'boys' night out'. It's crazy,

man, and I'm not ashamed to admit it 'cause I've said it before. You're the first man I've ever loved, Hugh."

"You know my dad always taught me that to love a man is to be a man, and I didn't know what he meant at the time, but he was right … and thank the muses. My coaches preferred teaching how to be competitive, how to sublimate feelings in secret handshakes and wrestling and aggression on the court—"

"Don't get me started with the military," Slim responded. "What is it about this here world that teaches men to fear intimacy and vulnerability?"

"Boys will be boys," Hugh concluded. "And girls will be girls, and so the binary world goes round and round. I wonder when we'll ever start talking about humans again."

"It's almost as bad as saying boyfriend and girlfriend!" Slim added. "How is it possible that middle schoolers use the same term as adults in their fifties?"

"Well, that's a question for both of you," I suggested. "What do y'all think it means to be a man?"

"Being a man is what we're doing right now," Slim didn't hesitate. "Cooking and philosophizing and drinking whiskey—like you said, simply acting like a halfway human being."

"No, I mean more like an adjective, though. What does it mean to be a man? Give me three words."

"An adjective?" Slim said. "That's easy. Self-respect."

"You're going to need to elaborate …"

"No, I won't. I mean *self-respect*, plain and simple. How do you expect to respect someone—or be respected by any-one, for that matter—if you don't respect yourself first and foremost? A world without respect? That's not a world I want to live in."

"Fair enough. I wouldn't put that first, though," Hugh said. "Self-respect can turn into arrogance. You respect yourself too much, and you start looking down on other people. Then it turns into the opposite of what you're talking about, right?"

"Well, shit," Slim answered. "I didn't know these adjectives were ranked. I have to say which one I'm putting first, now?"

"No, they don't have to be ranked," I said.

"My first choice is 'honesty'," Hugh pondered. "And I'm not just talking about honesty and having good morals and whatnot, I mean being honest with yourself. Maybe what I mean is integrity, though. You know, in Latin, integrity means the quality of being whole. It comes from integer, entire—"

"Here we go, Lockart!" Slim laughed. "We're gonna need a few beers for this conversation. Hugh's always trying to impress me with his Latin roots and shit. You think the origin matters? I don't give a flying fuck where the word came from as long as I understand it—"

"You know as well as I do that's just wrong," Hugh replied and cracked open a bottle of beer. "Origins are everything."

"All I'm saying is, I don't need a Latin lesson to understand what you're talking about. Cheers to that!" Slim raised his bottle to mine and Hugh's.

CLINK

"What about the second adjective then?" I asked.

"That's easy," Slim replied first. "Toughness. A man who isn't tough? Life will break you. Better men than you and I have been broken by heavy shit. I know, I know—it's a cliché—a masculine answer—but shit, when did it become a crime to try and talk about the virtues of masculinity?"

"Yeah, but forgive me, Slim," Hugh said. "I don't think you mean what you're saying. Toughness … I don't know, there are plenty of people who endure pain because they're tough, but it doesn't mean toughness leads to decency. I'd go with determination, being able to stick to a task, believing in yourself, but once again, check out the root—give me shit, I don't care—it's Latin for limiting something, fixing something, setting boundaries. You have to know your limits; you have to determine your boundaries—"

"And other people's boundaries, too," Slim agreed. "Determination is good, but I'm sticking with toughness. You can be determined as shit, but if you aren't tough? Good luck when the bullets start flying. You know where I'd be if it weren't for toughness? Hung up and tortured like those Blackwater idiots in Iraq. Or, but wait, they changed the name from Blackwater, didn't they?"

"Xe."

"Zee?"

"Xe."

"See?"

"X. E. Xe."

"Well, whatever they're called, Erik Prince is a determined piece of shit," Slim said. "He deserves to be bitch-slapped and locked up. But no, Hugh, you've gotta be tough if you want to be a man. There's no way around it."

"Agree to disagree," Hugh shook his head. "So I've got honesty and determination. And you've got self-respect and toughness. What about the third one?"

"I should've put this one at the top," Slim said. "Loyalty is everything. It's definitely more important than being tough or being honest. No, loyalty is number one. Without loyalty, I'd be nowhere 'cause remember, Hugh, loyalty also means being loyal to yourself. That's intuition. My father—whoever the fuck he is or was—wasn't loyal for shit. He left me alone to be raised by Wilhelmina. But you know why I stuck it out with moms and Stoke Ridge? I was loyal to my principles. When I make a decision, I stick to it."

"Loyalty's good," Hugh was pensive. "But I'm going with humility. And especially because I know you'll love to learn the etymology of the word, Slim: humus comes from the idea of being earthbound, like, literally low to the ground—down to earth. If you want to be a fulfilled man, woman, or anything in between—we're only ever talking about humans, after all—first and foremost, you better be humble. So I've got honesty, determination, and humility, and you've got self-respect, toughness, and loyalty. I like it. Not bad. What about you, Lockart? What makes a man?"

"You know, Jane has this philosophy she calls the three Ps: being passionate, patient, and making a concerted effort to be present. And that's as close to a complete human as one could be."

"Passion, patience, and presence," Slim repeated. "I reckon I can get behind those, too."

"Agreed," Hugh said. "How about we get started on the cooking?"

"I know for a fact I've got a couple of pounds of grass-fed beef. Will that do?"

"Frozen or refrigerated?"

"What kind of cook do I look like, Slim?"

"Ha!" Slim put his hand on my shoulder. "Well, I don't know, Lockart. Sometimes frozen meat can be alright. What matters is how you prepare the burger. Let's get down to business, Lockart. As you know, when it comes to burgers, I'm pretty precise about my system. Just like rolling joints, I like 'em how I like 'em, so first thing's first: do you have any—"

"Texas Pete," Hugh finished Slim's sentence.

"No way, man! That comes at the end!" Slim laughed. "First, find me a crisp head of lettuce, sliced tomatoes, avocados, the fixings for coleslaw, eggs, American cheese, ketchup, and *then* we can think about the hot sauce—like Hugh said, Texas Pete, to be precise."

As I checked the storage fridge to confirm the ingredients, Slim and Hugh bobbed their heads to an album I'd never heard of, a mash-up of Notorious BIG and Frank Sinatra called *Blue Eyes Meets Bed-Stuy*. I had to scrounge for the avocados—Jane always insisted we have a few on-hand for guacamole—and brought out all the fixings in addition to three fresh bottles of beer.

CRACK

A gust of wind seemed to slip under the bar's roof, sending a shudder through the building's frame.

"Hot damn!" Slim laughed. "We're about to be carried away like Dorothy!"

Hugh cleared a space on the kitchen island for cutting

the vegetables. "You got potatoes, Lockart?"

"Of course." I brought him a few spuds from the pantry.

"We'll bake them in the oven," Hugh explained. "But first we'll have to blanch them. Then we'll dress them with some garlic and rosemary, put them on a baking sheet, and drizzle some olive oil on top before popping them in the oven. Slim, in the meantime, you can caramelize a couple of onions."

"You boys don't mess around," I chuckled as I put the potatoes in a pot, filled it with water, and handed them two tall glasses of water to accompany their beers. "Before you guzzle down another beer, you gotta stay hydrated. Two for one—that's Jane's rule, and you don't mess with Jane. Chug it if you want to, just make sure you drink the water before the second beer."

Hugh's voice was tender. "It's the same reason my dad insisted we always eat bread with dried Spanish meats—to properly savor things. You're a wise man, Lockart. Hey, Slim, drink up. If we have too much beer, we won't have enough room for dinner. Delayed gratification, you know how it works."

Slim downed the water and raised his empty glass. "Here's looking out for *you*, too, Hugh."

"Ah, that reminds me," Hugh reached into his pocket and pulled out a Ziploc bag filled with green and yellow pills. "Vitamins."

"What kind of vitamins?" I pointed at the green pills with yellow dots.

"Wellness Formula," Hugh replied. "My mom swore by it. It helps with just about everything."

Slim rolled his eyes. "Yeah, right … only if you believe in it."

Hugh smiled. "You gotta put your faith in something, right?"

"You're not wrong," Slim conceded. "Hey, Lockart. Why don't you put on some music next? I can do it for you. What would you like to hear?"

Slim worked his magic with the Bluetooth speaker and soon Cannonball Adderley's *Somethin' Else (Rudy Van Gelder Edition)* filled the kitchen.

"Hugh, how about a little bit of weed? A little pregame spliff for cooking?" Slim pulled out a perfectly rolled joint. "Just a couple of puffs for now, though, we don't want to blast *too* far away."

Slim lit the joint and closed his eyes, and the image sent me back to a different time—a time of youth. I watched the tip of the joint glow orange to the soundtrack of Miles on the trumpet. We were at peace. I felt like a kid again.

"It's been years since I've smoked," I admitted. "I didn't know you youngsters still rolled joints with tobacco. Pass that spliff over when you're done."

Hugh took his two puffs and passed the joint to me.

"Remember when we got so high you had to take care of me?" Hugh exhaled a plume of smoke. "And you had to keep telling me I was fine and not to freak out?"

Slim laughed. "You were blazed out of your mind— probably gave you too big a hit."

"I've never been so terrified in my life," Hugh said. "I hadn't smoked weed since the beginning of the season, and Slim made me take a full bong hit! Man, I swear to God, I thought I was going to be *that guy*, you know? Destined for the NBA and then boom—smokes some weed and he ruins his life. Not that weed can kill you, but still, I freaked out. Remember how I had to sit in that chair? I couldn't move at all, and I remember you told me to sit down, and you made me some tea. You made sure I didn't lose my shit. A good friend, indeed."

Slim smiled. "He was high as a kite, Lockart. He didn't realize sometimes it's okay to lose control—to be that far gone."

"Well," Hugh reminisced. "That might have been the first time I felt safe enough around someone other than my parents."

We smoked the spliff and for a time didn't feel the need to converse as Cannonball Adderley took us out of the bar and up through the storm clouds through sheets of gray rain, the saxophone taking us higher still, towards some kind of bliss, approaching the calm of the eye of the storm where the wind dissipated, and then the song began to sing a sadder tune once more, residing in a minor key for a time, until the piano solo brought us back down to where we could sit in shared silence and relish in our separate peace.

"Man," Hugh said. "That's one of the most beautiful songs I've ever heard."

"I'm glad you liked it," I smiled. "Cannonball and Miles and Art Blakey on the drums. Sam Jones on the bass. Hank Jones on the keys? You can't go wrong."

"The weed doesn't hurt either!" Slim laughed. "Sorry to keep changing the music, Lockart, but do you mind if I put on the next song?"

"Young people these days … there was a time people respected the album, not just the song. Sure, go ahead, but let's listen to the entire album. Choose wisely."

Slim did his manipulations with his gadget. "We have a tradition to start Boys' Night with the El Michels Affair. Have you heard of it? Listen to that hi-hat! I can't get enough of it. This Isaac Hayes tribute album will set the right tone for the rest of the night."

As the music picked up, we took charge of the cooking island. Hugh unwrapped the burger meat and tossed it into a metallic mixing bowl. Slim knew his way around the kitchen without even asking, too; was soon sprinkling powdered garlic, curry, and a pinch of cumin into the bowl, finally adding a dash of olive oil and a bit of balsamic vinegar to the mix.

"We'll mix it all in just nice like." Slim picked up an avocado and squeezed it in his palm. "Perfect texture. Not too hard, not too soft. Speaking of, Hugh, how was your last night with Jessica?"

Hugh laughed as he began to mix the burger meat with the other ingredients. "It was okay. It wasn't the first time we hooked up, though. I was seeing her right around Christmas, remember? And the first couple of times we had sex, it was a bit awkward, to be honest . . ."

The music's horn section picked up as Slim tossed the avocado between his hands. "That's no surprise. The first time can be awkward, especially if you're drunk. Sometimes, I think making love is like breaking in a new pair of shoes."

"So you're saying you get blisters?" Hugh joked. "But

yeah, it can take a bit of time to get in sync. Plus, she'd just broken up with her boyfriend, so she wasn't really *there* mentally, you know? She didn't seem fully present."

Slim went to the pantry and returned with a carton of eggs, cracking one over the sink, careful to discard the egg whites, transferring the yolk from one half of the shell to the other.

"This is the secret to a good burger, Lockart," Slim poured the yolk into Hugh's mixing bowl. "It adds consistency. You know something, Hugh? I'm not proud to admit it, but I still haven't had sober sex."

Slim started chopping cabbage for the coleslaw. "But you know, it's hard to be present when your mind isn't there. And you know what I hate? When girls—young women, sorry—ask me, *are you going to cum*, as if I could just do it on command—as if I even wanted to. What would happen if I asked them the same question? It isn't cool to put that kind of pressure on a first date. And these girls—can you call them women if they can't fuck? I don't think so—these young college girls, well, if they can't *also* make me feel at ease, and especially if alcohol is involved, it's just not happening. Lockart, can you pass me the onion?"

"And you better believe I've faked it," Slim said as he sliced the onion in half, cutting it vertically, following the lines, deep enough to sever but not enough to separate. "Expecting me to have an orgasm without making me feel comfortable? No. I'm not into that."

Slim used the edge of the knife blade to swipe diced onions into Hugh's mixing bowl. "Come on now!" He continued. "You better believe I'll be shaking and quaking if it's the difference between having to keep pretending and going to sleep. Girls don't have hegemony over fake orgasms … like Kramer said, sometimes it's enough already and you just wanna get some sleep … you just gotta make sure you take off the condom quickly and hide it in the trash; I learned the hard way trying to flush a condom down a toilet."

"I've faked it once or twice, too," Hugh admitted.

"Because you wanted to go to sleep?"

"No. The truth is, I was bored and hungry," Hugh said. "It was during sophomore year in the dorms. I was having sex with this young woman—okay, girl—whose name I can't even remember, and I could hear people announcing free slices of pizza out in the hallway. I knew she didn't want to be there either—both of us were just too drunk—and it just felt like it was time to stop. She ended up eating pizza with me, though. Aside from the sex, she was actually really cool."

"So you got up and ate the pizza?"

"Well, it's not like we jumped out of bed immediately—I pretended to shake and quake first. But yes. I faked an orgasm for pepperoni pizza. I don't regret it. Lockart, can you pull out the other burger fixings from the fridge?"

I abided and went to the fridge for slices of American cheese—the industrial kind, wrapped in cheap plastic, which I removed oh-so-carefully, making sure not to rip it, laying the squares on a plate to reach room temperature.

"… but Jessica came twice the last time we slept together," Hugh was saying. "I was seriously proud."

"And how do you know she wasn't faking?" Slim asked.

"Because my head was between her legs and I felt the contractions, and let's just say there was … physical proof."

"No way!" Slim said. "I'm not a fan of female ejaculate. It's too musky."

"Oh, I love it. But to each his own," Hugh said. "I love seeing the fruits of my labor, you know what I mean? Men don't have hegemony over ejaculating, either. But if I can be honest, when I think about Jessica, it's not the sex I remember so much as cuddling up for a nice movie or holding hands walking down Franklin Street … Lockart, those potatoes should be ready now if you want to take them off the stove."

I drained the blanched potatoes into a colander and poured them onto a baking sheet, which Hugh drizzled with olive oil and topped with powdered garlic and fresh rosemary.

I prepared the burger buns for grilling while Slim sautéed caramelized onions and described his latest exploits.

"… her looks got the best of me, I'll admit it. On our second date, we went through a couple of bottles of red wine and got into a heated debate about how famous artists—Amy Winehouse in particular—have to conduct themselves differently than us regular folk."

"How do you reckon?" I asked.

"What I mean is, people look up to celebrities differently, and if you're going to become famous, you've got to accept that responsibility—you're a role model, you know? You can't have the fame and fortune without accountability. Anyway, our debate led to some heavy petting, and soon enough, we got down to business, but she kept breaking the rhythm and complaining about how much she hated condoms. I said I agreed but that, you know, it's better we be safe, and she got mad at me for refusing to take off the condom, so we stopped fucking for a few minutes, and then she came back to me and asked to start again. Lemme tell you, it was damn confusing. So I put on another condom, and once again, she started saying how she couldn't feel anything with condoms—as if I could feel any better!—and how skin-on-skin contact is the only way to really be *intimate* with someone. But still, I didn't want to take the risk—both of us had been sleeping around—so I refused to take the condom off, and then—to this day, I have no idea how she did it—all of a sudden, the sex felt amazing. She'd slid the condom off without me noticing. It was honestly quite impressive."

"You haven't told me this one before!" Hugh said. "So you're saying she assaulted you."

"Well, no. That's not assault. I was already inside of her. Bamboozled me, sure. Put my dick in danger, of course—"

"So what'd you do?"

"What anyone else would do—I started touching myself just next to her, saying I was about to cum, because obviously I wasn't going to take that risk, and that's when she blew up at me, saying how dare I fuck her without a condom but not want to finish inside of her, saying 'you men are all the same' and proceeding to pour a tall glass of cold water over *both of us* in the bed."

"What?"

"Yeah. There was a literal puddle of water between us—we were drenched. And the worst part is, I saw her again a year later, and she asked me out again, and you can take a guess what old twenty-one-year-old Slim did: he slept with her again."

"Jesus."

"Yeah. I got tested, though. I was fine. And lord, her mind was all over the place, but her body was damn sexy. She represented the epitome of what I'd always been taught a woman *should be*—buxom, bodacious, luscious, you know the rest of it. Anyway, I learned my lesson. I think these caramelized onions are done."

"Did you turn off the stove?" Hugh asked.

"Yeah, I did."

"Check again. Always double-check. I think we're almost good to go. I'm going to make the coleslaw now. Maybe you can get ready to fry the eggs?"

"Can do," Slim abided as Hugh filled a stainless-steel mixing bowl with mayonnaise, white vinegar, the chopped cabbage, some caramelized onions, black pepper, sea salt, a finely chopped Granny Smith apple I'd been working on, and a splash of Calvados from an old bottle I'd found at the bar—a gift from Jane's friends in Paris.

While Hugh told me about his parents' dream to retire in Paris, Slim grabbed a fistful of meat from the mixing bowl and formed it into a burger patty, pressing his thumb into the meat to create a slight indentation in the center, lining six burgers up on the wax paper.

"They'll puff up otherwise," Hugh said. "This way they'll stay flat. Lockart, can you splash some water on those buns, too? We don't want them to dry out. That cheese looks room-temperature enough now to put it on the buns and throw them in the oven."

"Hold up, Hugh! Don't put on the cheese just yet," Slim insisted. "I'm not trying to have hot cheese drip down on my hands. You know I got a second-degree burn from a goddamned Hot Pocket? See that mark next to my right thumb?"

As the potatoes baked in the oven, with only the burgers and the eggs left to cook on the stove, we went to the back porch to check up on Beverly.

Black clouds pelted the back yard with penny-sized raindrops, carving out torrential streams and miniature ponds in the garden.

"I want to *feel it*. Just real quick," Hugh proposed venturing out into the yard. "I loved watching hurricanes as a kid. Just a quick step outside."

"Not a good idea, Hugh."

"I'm literally taking one step out. Just to see what it's like. Come with me, Slim. Why not?"

Despite my protests, Slim and Hugh stepped into the breach. The gusts of wind would've blown lighter men clean off their feet. Hugh continued walking towards the forest edge whilst Slim stayed behind, calling out flying debris.

As leaves and tree branches swirled above Hugh's head, cracks of lightning illuminated the hurricane sky swirling above. Hugh crouched low like a weather reporter and was nearly hit by a flying tree branch on his return.

As he doubled back, pine cones and pine needles battered his shoulders. "What a storm!" He was grinning. "Did you see that branch? It almost smashed me in the face! Man, what a rush. Let's make sure the kitchen is clean before we finish up—that's the mark of a good chef, you know—and then we can get those burgers on the stove."

We tidied up the kitchen island, wiped down the counter tops, and continued the conversation over cold beers.

"… the bottom line is moderation," Slim was saying as he carried the tray of burger buns towards the stove. "Like tonight—we're tipsy and a bit high, but we're not drunk. It's not like we *need* weed to enjoy this … but it's also nice to let loose and welcome the Dionysian inside all of us."

"Knowing when to stop is the key," Hugh said. "Anyway, when I think of weed, I don't think of partying. Weed remains the cheapest vacation I know … or maybe not so much vacation as a return to myself."

Hugh turned on the gas stove but kept the flame low. "I want to make sure the pan gets nice and hot first. You want it to sizzle when you place the meat. Yep, I'm definitely high now."

"That makes three of us," I laughed. "I'm enjoying the ride."

"Can you pass me a smaller pan, Lockart?" Slim asked. "For the eggs? For me, weed isn't *only* about escapism. It definitely plays into that mindset—I mean, that's what's scary about a bad high, right? Escaping reality only to find yourself in a different world you don't want to be in. Like a stranger in your own novel—"

"That's it!" Hugh exclaimed. "Like a fly on the wall of your own life. Even now, just a second ago, I thought, *Fuck, am I too high? Am I going to ruin this night because I got too high and I'm going to have to pretend to be someone I'm not?* But of course I know I'm fine because I'm with you, Slim. And that's what

Jane meant, right? To be able to enjoy the ride?"

"Yes indeed. You've *got to be present.*"

Slim raised his beer. "I can cheers to that. And to something else: this man's going to be a top-ten pick!"

Hugh kept an eye on the heating frying pan. The butter mixed in with the olive oil began to brown at the edges.

"Yeah. Top-ten pick … I don't know about that. I still sometimes wonder if—"

"Oh, not this again," Slim shook his head. "Take the money and run, Hugh. We've talked about this. Are you telling me you want to watch oil heat for the rest of your life and sit around drinking with me?"

"Well, yeah, so what if I do? Would that be so wrong? It's what I've been trying to tell you, Slim—it's more complicated than that. There are contracts and papers and things to wrap up with my settlement with Coach Brees … it's not just about going to the NBA or not."

"Well shit." Slim clasped his hands together. "For the sake of argument, let's say it isn't your thing, the NBA. What are we talking about then? You're a seven-foot college basketball legend with a bachelor's degree. You might get a documentary out of it, sure, and yes, I agree you're a formidable cook, but what are we talking about, here? You want to be a professional chef? You don't have the constitution for cocaine, my friend. And without a bit of speed? That's an impossible industry. There ain't no shame in doing it for your parents—far from it—but isn't it possible you're idealizing their entire legacy now that they're gone? It's harsh, I know, Hugh, but I wouldn't be your friend if I weren't honest."

"But what if you're wrong? What if a chef *is* what I'm meant to be?"

"I could be wrong. Of course. But either way, the fact is, everything's always changing all the time, and I don't think you should skip out on a fat paycheck for a year or two. At least try it! Whatever you choose, it's going to be different from what you expect. That's life, my friend. The real question is, what are you willing to sacrifice?"

"You know," Hugh pulled the buns out of the oven, and placed a piece of crisp lettuce on the bottom bun, proceeding to pack down the coleslaw with the rounded edge of a spoon. "That reminds me of something Michael Jordan told the owner of the Chicago Bulls when Jordan broke his foot and the owner banned him from playing against the Celtics in the playoffs."

"What are we talking about MJ now? The dude is the GOAT!" Slim raised his voice. "The Greatest of All Time. The most passionate basketball player in the history of the game—"

"Exactly. And you know what happened when he broke his foot? He missed sixty-four games, and Jerry Reinsdorf, the owner, told him not to risk coming back too early for the playoffs. He said he had his whole career in front of him—get healthy before next season, he said—and still Jordan insisted on playing, and so Reinsdorf asked him the infamous question: imagine you've got a piercing headache—you can't even see straight—and someone hands you ten painkillers, one of which is coated in cyanide. Do you take the risk?"

"Hell no."

"That's not what Jordan said. Jordan said it depends on how bad the headache is. And a couple of weeks later, Jordan chose to play, and he set a playoff scoring record that still stands to this day. Sixty-three points against Larry Bird in Boston Garden. Passion overrides everything, Slim—*that's* what I'm saying—and it just so happens that maybe my passion is no longer for the game. Maybe it never was."

"Okay, fine. Now don't get defensive—I'm not calling you out, Hugh—but you can't afford to leave the game. Not now. I know, I know, but you know what I mean. You've got a responsibility to take advantage of the opportunity. At least clear your name with Coach Brees first."

Hugh shook his head. "You're not listening. Look."

Hugh grabbed a napkin. "Do you have a pen, Lockart? Thanks. Here, I'll write it out for you: in Jordan's first *nine years*—eight, really, because he missed most of his second year—here's what he did. Also, Lockart, would you mind grabbing me another beer?"

Hugh was determined. He wrote like a curious student, his tongue tucked into the side of his mouth, his mind trying to find the answer to an equation:

<u>The First Nine Years</u>
- Rookie of the Year
- 2 Olympic golds
- 2 slam dunk championships
- '88 Defensive Player of the Year
- All-Defensive 1st Team '88–'93
- All-Star '85–'93 (never <u>wasn't</u> an All-Star)
- Scoring Champ '87–'93
- 3 MVPs ('88, '91, '92)
- 3 Championships, 3 Finals MVPs

"And Jordan did all of this—*all of it*—before he was thirty. Now you can look at this and say, yeah-okay-he-was-a-great-player-maybe-the-greatest-of-all-time-big-deal—Chamberlain was also legendary, and Bill Russell, and Magic versus Larry and Kobe and LeBron, et cetera. But this is why Jordan beats them all, and it's not because of this napkin or all the other napkins I'd need to write down his legacy, because the *real heroics* can't be quantified, Slim—they can't be summarized on a piece of paper."

"I'm confused," Slim said. "So what are you saying?"

"The reason Jordan is the Greatest of All Time has almost nothing to do with basketball. In 1993—"

"You mean, after the first three-peat?" Slim cut in. "Man, that definitely was legendary. He had to go through Ewing and Starks and Wilkins and Price and Daugherty and Jordan Rules Chuck Daly and Pat Riley—and poor Craig Ehlo, not to mention facing off against Barkley. He was a giant killer, I get it. Okay. Point taken. But you're saying there's something else—"

"You're not listening, Slim. Let me finish. It's not about the game. It's about Jordan's life. His dad was the most important man in his life. James Jordan wasn't just a father figure; he was Michael's mentor, his best friend, always the first one to hug him after the championship game. And in the summer of ninety-three, after the third championship, James Jordan was murdered on the highway in his brand-new car—robbed and shot in a car his son had bought him as a gift after winning his third NBA championship. Two months later, Jordan retired from the game, and just like that, the greatest basketball player in history—at the height of his career, mind you—called it quits. And, of course, conspiracy theories started about how James was assassinated, about MJ's supposed gambling problem, about his ties to the mafia—anything for a story—and when the media tried to profit, how do you think the most famous person in the world chose to respond? He questioned his motivations for everything. He had to think of a new reason to exist, and for that, he had to step away from basketball. See, his dad always told him he could do anything he set his mind to, and the bottom line was Jordan needed a change. A chapter had ended, albeit in a horrific way, and it was time to move on to something else. James Jordan had always thought Michael could be a professional baseball player—not because he'd be great but because it'd be a challenge."

"*That something's difficult must be another reason to do it.* Rilke said that…" Slim replied.

"Exactly. And so when James died, Michael took a chance and started playing baseball in the minor leagues so he could remember what it felt like to play for the love of the game."

"He needed to find his passion again…" Slim was starting to understand. As the fried eggs simmered in the buttery skillet, he used the spatula to carefully brown the edges.

"Exactly! And Jordan said it himself," Hugh replied. "Don't break the yolk—yeah, nice. You know, someone once said Jordan wasn't addicted to gambling—he was addicted to his passion for competition. Even before his dad died, Jordan had been struggling to find passion in basketball. When it came to his accomplishments, there was nothing else for him to achieve; Jordan even broke down in Coach Phil Jackson's office trying to come up with a new challenge. He'd won championships and MVPs and defensive awards and gold medals—he was called even back then, even before the second threepeat, the greatest player to ever play—and he couldn't think of a worthy reason to keep playing the game. So where do you go from there, Slim? Where do you go when you're empty?"

"But you're not empty, Hugh, not yet," Slim said.

"I might be emptier than you think. But what I'm saying is, Jordan became a legend precisely because he dared to step away. It wasn't a wise choice professionally, but it was a wise choice existentially. And when he tried baseball, which is one of the hardest sports in the world to play, by the way, he failed miserably. Have you seen that documentary, *Jordan Rides the Bus*? He struck out, over and over again. He was the laughingstock of the entire sports world. He was called a joke, a fraud, an over-hyped athlete seeking attention. He was called an egomaniac who wanted to hog the spotlight … but instead of listening to all the noise, you know what he did? Jordan just kept playing. And he kept getting better. Day in and day out, he practiced— scouts say he was the most driven player on the team—and soon he began to show signs of not only holding his own but *succeeding*. The thing is, Slim, Jordan retired from the NBA to prove something to himself; by refusing to become a washed-up player whose passion would inevitably fade away, Jordan retired in 1993 because he knew a life without passion isn't a life worth living."

"Well shit, Hugh …" Slim said.

"I'm not finished. You can probably turn the flame off and cover them; the residual heat will do the rest. So Jordan came back full of love in 1995 and returned in incredible form. Fifty-five points in Madison Square Garden in a play-off game. The man is an absolute basketball legend. But his success wasn't immediate, and against the Orlando Magic, he committed two critical turnovers that cost the Bulls the series, and once again, what do you think the world started saying about him?"

"That number forty-five would never be as good as number twenty-three."

"Exactly. They attacked him again, like they always do. People don't want to see legends succeed—they want to see legends fall. And sure, he was pissed and disappointed, but he'd also found what he was looking for—not the talent, but the motivation—and lo and behold, Jordan ended up leading the greatest team in sports history to a fourth championship—seventy-two wins in eighty-two games. That's unheard of. That's just stupid. And then he won *two more*. Now tell me, Slim, do you still think the point is 'success' over passion?"

"Your friend's got a point," I couldn't help but be impressed with Hugh's line of thinking.

"I'm not going to argue against passion," Slim replied. "All I'm saying is—"

"Oh, I'm not finished yet," Hugh smiled. "I think it's time for these burgers to go on the stove."

Hugh delicately placed each patty on the skillet and relished in the sizzle.

"We'll cook them a few minutes on each side—Slim, you can use that spoon to baste them with the butter. Yeah, just like that. So fast forward to the second time Jordan retired in 1998 after a *second* threepeat. Everyone wanted

Jordan's iconic shot against the Utah Jazz to be the final image—the Last Shot was a perfect ending—but we all made the mistake of thinking Jordan's story was supposed to be *our* happy ending."

"The Wizards. That was a choice," Slim was dubious. "Why join one of the worst teams in NBA history?"

"Who knows? Does it matter? Once again, Jordan wanted to prove something to *himself,* not us. And he did. He became one of the oldest players in history to score forty-plus points in a game. He was *the only player* in 2002 to play all eighty-two games of the season. And here's the icing on the cake: in the end, he disappointed all of us, inevitably. Did you see his Hall of Fame speech? Michael Jordan is a flawed human being like all the rest of us. Now he desperately wants to win as executive for the Charlotte Bobcats, and he's failing miserably. But that's what it takes when you choose to pursue passion—it means sacrificing your idea of yourself in pursuit of the capital-T truth about existence—"

"And what's that?" Slim asked.

"If you listen closely to the video in 1998," Hugh's eyes lit up. "After Game Six, after Jordan has just won the championship, he hugs Phil and says, 'I had faith, I had faith.' And *that's* what matters, Slim—having *faith* in ourselves. Faith to be whoever, whatever, and however we want to be."

"Well, for what it's worth, I have faith in you, Hugh." Slim hugged his friend. "Those burgers look mighty tasty. I think it's about time we eat. Lockart, you got the avocados? Ohhhh baby. Yeah, let's place them on the lettuce just nice like that. Then come the tomatoes and the onions, and all that's left are the condiments—to each his own."

"These burgers are huge!" Hugh was proud. "Let's spear them with steak knives to maintain their integrity."

Each of us carried our own plate to the bar's counter top and took a moment to gaze upon the fruits of our labor. I remember I sat down to the right of Slim, and on his left sat his best friend; Slim removed the steak knife along with the top bun and doused it all in Texas Pete.

14

Eye of the Storm

I don't remember which song was playing. For a time, we didn't speak, barely so much as glancing up from our plates, only occasionally resurfacing for a sip of beer.

Midway through our meal, cocooned by the sound of the rain, Slim put down his half-eaten burger and exclaimed, "One of the best Boys' Nights yet! I think it's about time for a whiskey!"

BOOM

Beverly had other plans. A thunderclap bellowed from the churning skies above and shook the bar down to the floorboards. The serenity disappeared along with the lights. A gust of wind blasted the front door open. Slim shoved me and Hugh to the ground, telling us to take cover like he was back in Iraq, instinctively crawling on his forearms towards the front door. The bar quaked and the lights flickered as a seam in the sky ripped in two, pouring white lightning into the bar. Outside, we could see sheets of rain floating across the parking lot, the floodwaters eddying on the churning ground as the pine trees buckled and twisted, and the defoliated mulberry bushes tried to keep their heads above water.

"Holy shit," Hugh yelled after following Slim to the open front door. "Look at my Jeep."

The water was rising. A sizeable tree branch had fallen on the roof, and another was sticking out of the smashed passenger window.

"Goddammit!" Hugh cursed. "The whole car's going to flood. I gotta get my bag out of there before it's too late."

"Are you serious, Hugh?" Slim screamed. "Who gives a shit about the bag? Look outside! Those are gale-force winds … you're not about to risk your life!"

The wind dislodged the Jeep's wheels from the muddied ground, and it began to slide ever so slightly across the flooded parking lot. "I've gotta get my bag, Slim. You don't understand. It's going to flood through the window—"

"Brother, wait it out. The eye's going to come soon enough. Look at the clouds, Hugh. Just wait a second."

The white noise of the rain swept their words away as we watched Beverly consume everything in her path. A rogue mailbox flew into the scene and smashed one of the Jeep's side mirrors.

"I have to save my bag!" Hugh took a step forward.

"Hugh, no!" Slim held him back. "You're going to get yourself killed."

Another tree branch smashed through the back windshield and lodged itself in the red Jeep Cherokee's rear cabin.

"I'm getting my bag," Hugh said. "You're coming with

me, Slim. It's right there."

In an instant, Slim and The Beast were out laboring in the gale, crouching like war photographers, sticking their arms out for balance. They grabbed onto each other's hands as they turned their backs to the wind, walking sideways, battling the hurricane's fury, their broad shoulders deflecting leaves and small tree branches. Rain swirled around them as they made their way across the swamped ground; although the Jeep wasn't more than one hundred feet away, I could only make out their silhouettes by the time they reached it. Hugh struggled to open the driver's seat door before he dove in, and Slim had to battle with the howling air and the tree branches stuck in the backseat before he managed to crawl inside. The taillights shone orange, and for a moment, they just sat there before heading back towards the bar, bag in hand.

Slim remained crouched low to the ground. Hugh clutched his bag to his chest. And then, all of a sudden, light emerged from behind the tree line, and a patch of blue sky seeped out. And just like that, the howling stopped. They were caught in the perfect still, dumbfounded, squinting into the clear blue eye of the storm. Hugh put his arm around Slim and began plodding back to the bar, sloshing in puddles of mud like a rubber-booted kid. By the time they reached the front door, it seemed Beverly had disappeared entirely. No more thunder or lightning, only a gentle breeze. Hugh and Slim started to laugh. Branches settled into the mud. The pines stood up, shaking off the rain, stretching their limbs. The worst was still to come, but everything was calm. All three of us were like children who'd just witnessed a magic trick. I stepped outside to join them and marvel at the gyrating eye wall looming in the distance.

"It's not over yet, boys," I exclaimed. "We've still got burgers and beer waiting."

Hugh kept his arm around Slim as they headed back onto the porch.

Slim was the first to see it—a shadowy figure emerging from the tree line in the distance, a man sprinting towards all three of us with alarming speed, armed with a shotgun.

The yellow-toothed smile said it all. "It's time for dinner, Slim. What are we having?"

"Take it easy, man," Hugh instinctively stood in front of his friend.

"No, get back, Hugh," Slim stepped in front of Hugh. "Sgt. Dykes is mine now."

"So you've told him about me!" Dykes said. "Well, isn't that nice. Maybe we could all be friends! That is, if you have room for me, faggots."

Dykes led us inside with the barrel of the shotgun.

I whispered to Slim, "Don't do anything rash."

At the bar, Dykes poked at Hugh's chest with his gun. "Sit down on the stool. I've been waiting for you, Beast. That's what you are, isn't it? The world-famous Beast."

"What the fuck are you doing, Dykes?" Slim struggled to keep his composure.

"Now, now ... be patient, Slim. All in good time, my pretty."

"Chandler, please," I interjected. "You've—"

"Shut up, Lockart. I'm tired of hearing your shit. Sit

there, yeah, next to him. You too, Slim. And take off your shirt while you're at it."

Slim laughed. "You've got to be kidding me, Dykes! You're still a fucking freak. You'll have to shoot me first. Go ahead. You don't have the balls …"

"YOU WILL DO AS YOU'RE TOLD, SON! TAKE IT OFF! NOW!"

"Slim," Hugh spoke softly. "Just do it. It's not worth getting shot."

"What's that, Beast? What are you saying to your friend? Why don't you take your shirt off, too? Yeah, just like that. Maybe get on your knees, too."

Hugh and Slim reluctantly removed their T-shirts. All of their arm, chest, and back muscles were tense.

Hugh got on his knees first in front of the bar and put his hands atop his head.

"Oooh, look at you," Dykes said as he poked at Hugh's pecks with the gun. "Did Slim teach you the Stoke Ridge regimen? He used to be such a good cadet …"

"This is between us, not him," Slim lunged at the shotgun. Dykes recoiled.

"WHAT is between us, Slim? WHAT, exactly? Don't you mean this is between me and *him*?" Dykes pointed the gun at Hugh. "Now you're thinking. You fucking faggot."

Dykes was as drunk as I'd ever seen him, but there was a fury in his eyes that none of us could understand. He ripped a piece of paper out of his pocket and waved it in Hugh's face.

"Your friend here has been lying to you, Slim. Don't you want to know what happened? Don't you want to ask him about Coach Brees? How almost killing him went unpunished? Ask him why you're driving this piece of shit Jeep up to Milwaukee instead of flying. ASK HIM!"

"What the fuck are you talking about, Dykes? You're insane. Hugh, don't answer him."

"Beast? Why don't you tell him, hmm? I know your secret. You're a coward and a deserter *and* a faggot. GET UP."

"Hugh, don't answer him. Don't give him the satisfaction."

Dykes shrieked and jabbed the butt of the shotgun into Hugh's back. "FINE! I'LL DO IT MYSELF, LIKE ALWAYS. Stay on your knees, Beast! Get back down! Or no, why don't you do the honors, Lockart?"

Dykes slammed the paper on the bar and pointed the gun at me.

"READ IT!" Dykes bellowed.

I unfolded the piece of paper but refused to give Dykes the satisfaction. "I have no business with this. You'll have to read it yourself, Chandler."

Just a hint of fear flashed across his face.

"You're right," Dykes spoke quickly. "I'll do it myself. It's better like that. I had a nice little chat with Coach Brees the other day, Beast. He was mighty interested in that interview you gave ... seemed to be able to read between the lines. Don't want to go to the NBA, do you? Trying to get out of it? I did a bit of detective work myself, wondering why you were driving up to the draft. It sounds like you've been talking to scouts in Europe, too."

Something flickered in Hugh's eyes, but he remained calm.

"If you're going to point that at someone, point it at me," Slim pleaded.

"Slim, it's going to be okay," Hugh responded.

"You're damn right it's going to be okay!" Dykes screeched. "Well, maybe not for you. Coach Brees' lawyer is good, you know. Very good indeed. He has all the answers. I just had to figure out how to talk to him. What's in the bag, Beast? Why don't you ask him, Slim? Your *best friend* is trying to run away. He's going to abandon you. He's a coward, that's all."

Hugh remained silent.

"Point that at me, you pathetic piece of shit!" Slim grabbed the barrel of the gun and placed it squarely in his chest.

"Yeah, that's good," Dykes said. "But don't be mad at me. Ask him, Slim. Ask him why he bought two tickets. The private detective said one of them is in a girl's name. But you can't do that, can you, Beast? These are different times. Still have mommy and daddy's credit card, though. Do you miss them? How sad. All that education and you forgot they can track the credit card ..."

Hugh had nothing to say.

"It seems your *best friend* here is afraid to talk," Dykes sniggered. "So I guess I'll speak for him, just like always. You weren't going to take I-40 through Greensboro, were you, Beast? You were planning to flee to Atlanta. An international flight with your sweetie. What's her name again?"

Slim furrowed his brow skeptically. Hugh was visibly tense.

"Don't want to tell him, do you, Beast?" Dykes prodded.

"What are you, embarrassed? I'll tell him myself then. Beast here signed a contract last year, back when he punched Coach Brees. He was facing jail time. Oh, he didn't tell you that? That's because he's a liar. He cut a deal with the judge because he could only ever pay the damages with a future NBA contract. It's expensive to almost die, you know, not to mention psychological problems. Brees has been keeping an eye on him with a private investigator, and he even hired *me* to keep an eye on *you*. That's right, Beast: I've been following you. What a coincidence! What are the odds? You aren't allowed to leave North Carolina, are you? Wasn't that *also* part of the contract? Not until after the draft, at least. He lied to you, Slim. The Beast was never invited to Milwaukee. He has to stay inside the state until draft day, when he signs with a team, and *then* Coach Brees can reap twelve percent of the profits as his de facto agent! But you don't want to sign with a team, do you, Beast? What are you, scared? You're nothing without your nickname. You're nothing more than a stupid ballplayer, that's all. What, did you think Coach Brees would forget about it? That you could get out of paying him? All that education, and for what? Why did you sign the contract then? Too scared to go to jail? To be a nobody like your parents? The only reason he's with you, Slim, is 'cause he's using you to get out of town. Do you know what will happen if they catch him? You'll be tried as an accomplice. This is America. They'll hunt you down. The only thing better than succeeding is watching you fall. And you thought I was the problem! The oh-so-powerful Beast, signing away the rights to his own name instead of being a man and facing the music. And now you're trying to get out of it! That's where you're wrong. Your friend chose to sign the dotted line, Slim. The Beast is just a slave to the system like all the rest of them—part of the problem. What does that make you then, Beast? What do we call a man who signs his freedom away? And now you're fleeing? That sounds like cowardice to me! And what about you, Slim? What does that make you? Some kind of hostage? He used you, Slim. He's been lying to you since the beginning. Why do you think he made you his 'agent'—I bet you never signed any contract, did you? He was going to abandon you, Slim, just like everyone always does—just like your father."

For a moment, it seemed as if Slim's anger was shifting to his friend.

"Slim," Hugh's voice was weak. "Don't listen to him. I wasn't trying to use you, I promise. I got the bag out of the car because …"

A cruel smile stretched across Dykes' hateful face.

"No, Hugh," Slim's voice was assured. "It doesn't matter what this clown says. He's insane. He isn't worth the light of day. Don't give him the satisfaction. Right now, we need to deal with this piece of shit. Stand up, Hugh. We're not scared of him."

Slim stepped between Hugh and Sgt. Dykes. "Your plan didn't work, Dykes," he continued. "You fucking jackass conspiracy theorist. What did you think was going to happen? That I was going to believe you? That I was going to make Hugh the problem? You still don't get it, do you? You never got it. You're a pathetic excuse for a human being, and you're even less of a man than a human, so you better shoot me before I break your face!"

Slim grabbed the shotgun barrel and held it tight to his own chest. "You're going to shoot me? Is that how this goes down? I don't think you'll do it, Dykes. You're a goddamn coward. You think you can come in here with a made-up story and a piece of paper and take this all away? Go on then, pull the trigger. I'm not going to stop you."

Dykes' eyes flickered as if the demon inside had lit a match, and in the next instant, he pumped the shotgun and pulled the trigger.

The gun went *click*, but no bullets came out. Just a hollow, defeated silence.

Slim yanked the shotgun from Dykes' grasp and laughed in the sergeant's face. He threw the gun across the room. "We're going to need some rope, Lockart. This proud military man can't even load a shotgun correctly."

Slim cocked back his right fist and knocked Dykes to the ground.

Dykes stood up, but Hugh held Slim back. The sergeant blinked stupidly at the three of us and felt at the bridge of his broken nose. He pressed his hands to his eyes and touched the back of his bloodied head, wiping his bloodied palms on his khakis before raising his hands like a boxer and looking around wildly for a weapon; he settled on the steak knife next to Slim's half-eaten burger.

"Don't you fucking touch my burger!" Slim picked up a barstool and cocked it behind his head, but Hugh remained in front of Slim, preventing him from attacking.

Dykes began to advance slowly, clutching the bar to keep his balance, taking hold of one of the burger plates on the counter top and crashing it to the ground.

"You can't protect him, Beast. Just like you couldn't protect your parents."

Hugh's eyes widened. "What did you say to me?"

"Everybody knows you're the one who started that fire."

Dykes pointed the serrated steak knife at Hugh. "Stop hiding behind your boyfriend, Slim. For old time's sake: DROP AND GIVE ME TWENTY!" Dykes was all but foaming at the mouth. The rage had taken over. "Come around where Daddy can see you. I should've fucked you when I had the chance!"

Slim dropped the barstool and charged. Neither Hugh nor I could hold him back. All three fell to the ground, and in a matter of seconds, the scuffle was over. Dykes was unconscious on the floor, blood gushing profusely from his head. Slim stood up, brushed himself off, and gave Dykes one last kick to the ribs.

"Hugh, we got him."

But Hugh didn't speak. He was clutching his chest, writhing on the floor.

"Hugh?" Slim dropped to his knees. "Hugh, what the fuck happened!"

"Slim. . ."

Hugh looked down at the steak knife lodged deep next to his heart. He tried to sit up but couldn't manage.

Slim placed one hand under his friend's head. "Don't look at it, brother, you're fine."

Hugh coughed up blood. "Slim? What happened?"

He tried to prop himself up on his elbows but fell back down again. "Slim, listen to me. I want—"

"No, Hugh, don't talk like—"

"SLIM. *Please listen.* I was going to tell you. I promise I was. I just wanted to get out of here first. To leave it all behind. I bought a ticket for you, too. Everything we need is in my bag. I've got all the recipes, too. I was going to bring you with me. Chez Nous—"

"Don't talk, Hugh, you're fine. Lockart's calling an ambulance. Lockart! Call it now!"

"I was planning to tell you, Slim. I'm sorry. I didn't mean to—" Hugh's eyes widened as he coughed up more blood. "Slim? What's happening?"

Tears streamed down Slim's face. "You're fine, brother. Don't worry."

He caressed his friend's forehead and wiped his mouth. "You're fine, Hugh, it's nothing. You just stay right there. The ambulance is coming. Are you with me? We're going to be all right, I promise. Just keep breathing. Just like that. LOCKART! WHERE'S THE AMBULANCE!"

Slim wiped away his own tears. "That's it, brother. We're gonna be fine. Just keep pressing. Just like that. We're gonna be fine, brother."

But no ambulance was coming. Beverly wasn't finished. Hugh began to breathe heavily as the sunlight disappeared from the bar.

"It's like those snow globes when you're a kid," Hugh watched dust particles dance and glow in the dimming light. Slim looked at me with pleading eyes, but we both knew the eye wall was fast approaching. The sirens wouldn't come.

"You just stay right there, Hugh. You're fine. You're fine, Hugh. Don't worry."

Hugh's expression was serene. "Mom. Dad. This is it, isn't it?"

"No, brother, stop talking. You're going to be fine, just deep breaths."

"Slim," Hugh whispered. "It's okay. Just listen."

For a moment, there was only silence. Nothing but a calm breeze. And then the rain pattered on the roof, and the thunder and lightning rumbled, and an eerie sense of calm swept over the bar.

Hugh barely spoke above a whisper as he pulled his best friend close. "It's okay, Slim. Just listen." Hugh closed his eyes and exhaled.

For a moment, Slim remained draped over his friend before he fled into the howling winds.

Epilogue

They put The Beast in a body bag and Sgt. Dykes in a straitjacket. When they searched Chandler's cabin, they found a rabid opossum that was quickly put down. They put the B.A.M. LIST in a plastic bag and labeled it EVIDENCE.

B.A.M. LIST
~~Mom and Dad~~
Slim
~~General Haith~~
~~Saddam~~
~~The Facebook Team~~
~~The Beast~~
Me, Chandler Dykes

Hugh Dawton-Fields' ashes were scattered in James Taylor Creek and his jersey was hung up in the rafters of UNC's Dean Dome. An award-winning sports documentary entitled The Punch, The Beast, The Legend told quite the tragic story of an NBA career cut short, but only those who come to Lockart's learn about Hugh, and those who taste Slim's Famous Burger always ask about the name behind the legend.

"Slim's out there somewhere," I always respond, but your guess is as good as mine, 'cause the plain and simple truth is no one has seen or heard from Slim since. Some pundits like to pretend Slim had something to do with the killing, and others say Slim changed his name and became a philosopher abroad. The conspiracy theorists say Sgt. Dykes hired a former cadet, Toby, to hunt down Slim, and the most morbid of folks believe Slim must've committed suicide because there could be no Slim without The Beast.

But they're wrong. Everyone's entitled to their own opinion, but only the thoughtful are entitled to the truth—and the truth is, there's much more to a man than his upbringing or personal history—certainly much more than a bartender can surmise—and whoever Slim and The Beast were, or could have been, or hoped to become, it isn't as important as how we choose to remember them, now. Which is why I always tell folks who come out to Lockart's and learn about Hugh: as I watched him lying in his own pool of blood, all I could think of was that half-eaten burger: lettuce, coleslaw, sliced tomatoes, a burger patty, American cheese, avocado, a second patty, a fried egg, ketchup and hot sauce—Texas Pete to be precise.

To this day, here at Lockart's Bar, Slim's Famous Burger is the only burger on the menu, but during lunch hours, cooking with Jane, the bar goes by the name Chez Nous, inspired by the handwritten recipes Hugh left behind.

We all want to feel part of something real, something sacred, and something profound—like Slim once said, "in the past but not forgotten"—so when simple routines go to plan and we take the time to honor them, allowing each other to feel at ease and possess ourselves as we are, understanding that to love another is to first learn how to love yourself, well, I don't want to live in their past, but I want their past to live in me, and that's about all I've got to say about Hugh Dawton-Fields and a man named Slim.

THE END

SAMUÉL LOPEZ-BARRANTES is a writer and musician. He lives in Paris, where he leads historical walking tours on modernism, existentialism, and the Nazi Occupation. He sings and plays piano & harmonica alongside his twin brother, Aaron, and their dear friend, Aurelien, who they met on a Parisian basketball court. Their indie rock trio, Slim & The Beast, was named after this book. Lopez-Barrantes' second novel, *The Requisitions,* is also available from Kingdom Anywhere wherever books are sold.

samuellopezbarrantes.com
ifnotparis.substack.com
@samuellopezbarrantes

KINGDOM ANYWHERE is an independent anglophone
publisher in Paris, co-founded by
Lopez-Barrantes and Augusta Sagnelli.

Available Titles

The Requisitions (2024) - Samuél Lopez-Barrantes

SPILL: Poems (2025)- Mitalee Mehta

Slim and The Beast (2025)- Samuél Lopez Barrantes

Forthcoming Titles

A Tenative Gardener's Guide to the Evening: Poems -
John Sannaee

Please consider purchasing these titles
from your local bookstore.

kingdomanywhere.com

SLIM AND THE BEAST

www.ingramcontent.com/pod-product-compliance
Lightning Source LLC
Chambersburg PA
CBHW032313310726
48973CB00008B/2629